MUSIC IS THE SOUL OF LOVE

"You are not wearing your mask," he observed. He moved forward and stood looking down at her.

"No." Her lips barely moved.

She wondered if he would recognise her as the girl he had met years ago, on the night he was shot. Or perhaps the moonlight would make that harder. No recognition showed in his face as he gazed at her.

"You are very beautiful," he said fervently.

Then he put his arms around her and drew her closer to him. Almost before she realised what was happening, Carina felt his lips conquer hers.

As he drew her closer still, a strange feeling swept from her breast to her heart.

As the Duke's kiss held her captive, she thought for a moment she was flying up into the sky and touching the stars themselves.

He held her tighter and his kisses became more demanding so that she felt as if he was drawing her very heart from her body to make it his.

"So we reach the end of our games," he claimed huskily.

Carina tried to reply, but no words would come.

The Barbara Cartland Pink Collection

Titles in this series

MUSIC IS THE SOUL OF LOVE

BARBARA CARTLAND

Barbaracartland.com Ltd

THE BARBARA CARTLAND PINK COLLECTION

Barbara Cartland was the most prolific bestselling author in the history of the world. She was frequently in the Guinness Book of Records for writing more books in a year than any other living author. In fact her most amazing literary feat was when her publishers asked for more Barbara Cartland romances, she doubled her output from 10 books a year to over 20 books a year, when she was 77.

She went on writing continuously at this rate for 20 years and wrote her last book at the age of 97, thus completing 400 books between the ages of 77 and 97.

Her publishers finally could not keep up with this phenomenal output, so at her death she left 160 unpublished manuscripts, something again that no other author has ever achieved.

Now the exciting news is that these 160 original unpublished Barbara Cartland books are ready for publication and they will be published by Barbaracartland.com exclusively on the internet, as the web is the best possible way to reach so many Barbara Cartland readers around the world.

The 160 books will be published monthly and will be numbered in sequence.

The series is called the Pink Collection as a tribute to Barbara Cartland whose favourite colour was pink and it became very much her trademark over the years.

The Barbara Cartland Pink Collection is published only on the internet. Log on to www.barbaracartland.com to find out how you can purchase the books monthly as they are published, and take out a subscription that will ensure that all subsequent editions are delivered to you by mail order to your home.

If you do not have access to a computer you can write for information about the Pink Collection to the following address :

Barbara Cartland.com Ltd.
240 High Road,
Harrow Weald,
Harrow HA3 7BB
United Kingdom.

Telephone & fax: +44 (0)20 8863 2520

THE LATE DAME BARBARA CARTLAND

Barbara Cartland who sadly died in May 2000 at the age of nearly 99 was the world's most famous romantic novelist who wrote 723 books in her lifetime with worldwide sales of over 1 billion copies and her books were translated into 36 different languages.

As well as romantic novels, she wrote historical biographies, 6 autobiographies, theatrical plays, books of advice on life, love, vitamins and cookery. She also found time to be a political speaker and television and radio personality.

She wrote her first book at the age of 21 and this was called Jigsaw. It became an immediate bestseller and sold 100,000 copies in hardback and was translated into 6 different languages. She wrote continuously throughout her life, writing bestsellers for an astonishing 76 years. Her books have always been immensely popular in the United States, where in 1976 her current books were at numbers 1 & 2 in the B. Dalton bestsellers list, a feat never achieved before or since by any author.

Barbara Cartland became a legend in her own lifetime and will be best remembered for her wonderful romantic novels, so loved by her millions of readers throughout the world.

Her books will always be treasured for their moral message, her pure and innocent heroines, her good looking and dashing heroes and above all her belief that the power of love is more important than anything else in everyone's life.

"The tender words of love are as soft music to the ear."

- Barbara Cartland

CHAPTER ONE
1865

The theatre was abuzz. The performance of *Twelfth Night* was magnificent and soon it would be time for the lights to go down for the last act.

From her place in a box near the stage, fourteen-year-old Carina Denton sighed with delight. Her first visit to London had proved to be everything she had hoped and tonight was the best of all.

When her school friend, Alice Grade, had invited her for a visit, her parents had been a little uncertain. But Alice's family were respectable, old-fashioned people and permission was soon given.

"Alice, who is that?" Carina whispered to her friend, indicating a young man in the box immediately opposite.

He was in his early twenties, and incredibly handsome, Carina thought. Tall, elegant, striking and attired in full evening-dress, with cuff-links that must have been real diamonds from the way they sparkled.

But there was something else about him that drew her attention. His dark eyes were fierce and turbulent. His curved mouth hinted at a darkly sensual nature.

Not that Carina understood this. She only knew that there was a wildness and a drama about him that made it impossible for her to turn away.

"I don't know him," Alice whispered back.

"What are you girls whispering about?" asked Miss Ferrars, her governess.

"We are wondering who that young man is," Alice told her.

Miss Ferrars gave a little gasp and averted her eyes modestly.

"That is Lord Thornhill and you must not look at him."

"Why?" Carina wanted to know.

"Because he is not a proper person."

"Why?" Alice demanded.

Miss Ferrars was in an awkward position. As a governess she was expected to be prim, proper and puritanical at all times. Yet beneath the severe bodice of her dark dress beat the heart of a romantic.

Normally her employer, Alice's mother, would have answered these questions. But at the last minute Mrs. Grade had been stricken with a headache, and Miss Ferrars alone had accompanied the girls to the theatre.

"He is improper because – he does improper things," she said lamely.

"What sort of things?" Alice persisted. "Oh, do tell us please."

"He has a bad reputation," Miss Ferrars replied. "People say he is – dissolute."

"But what does he do?" Carina wanted to know.

Poor Miss Ferrars could not have answered that question in a million years. At forty she was as innocent and sheltered as a young girl. She knew that Lord Thornhill was dissolute because she had been told that he was. But precisely how a man went about being dissolute she had only the vaguest idea.

"Never mind," she said hastily. "Thank goodness he has gone now."

Lord Thornhill had slipped away through the curtains at the back of his box. Miss Ferrars gave a sigh of relief.

But her relief was to be short-lived. A moment later he appeared in the box immediately next to theirs.

Now Carina could see him better.

He was little more than a boy, although his face was already marked by experience. He had the air and grace of a prince who knew that the world was his to be enjoyed as he pleased.

Carina gazed at him, awed by his aura of glamour and romance, thinking that he was exactly what a hero ought to be.

The box beside them contained three ladies who, from their family resemblance, might have been a mother and two daughters.

He courted them all, kissing their hands, giving them practised, flirtatious smiles. The girls looked at him with yearning, the mother with knowing anticipation.

The door at the back of the box opened and a middle aged man came in. As soon as he saw Lord Thornhill, Carina could sense the tension.

'He does not like him,' she thought, watching the man's suspicious eyes flicker from his wife to his daughters. 'I wonder why?'

But however deep his dislike, the man evidently lacked the courage to order Lord Thornhill out of his box. As the lights went down for the last act, the young man settled himself audaciously between the daughters.

The curtain went up. In moments Carina was absorbed by what was happening on the stage, believing in the characters, loving every moment of it.

"Fiend!"

The voice rang out from the stage and everyone sat up, alert. There was something different about the man who had entered and was standing in the spotlight.

"Foul fiend! Vile seducer!"

A buzz went round the audience as people began to realise that this was not part of the play. The man who had rushed onto the stage was thin, gaunt and unshaven. His clothes were expensive but he looked as though he had slept in them.

He was pointing at Lord Thornhill as he screamed,

"Villain! Wretch! The world shall know you for what you are. No decent house should receive you. No woman is safe."

The young Lord had risen and come to the front of the box. Clearly he recognised himself in the accusation and was ready to brazen it out.

"Girls, it's time we were going," Miss Ferrars declared, all a-flutter.

"Oh no!" they protested in unison.

Lord Thornhill, standing just on the other side of the low divide, heard this and turned his blazing grin onto them.

"Ignore him, ladies," he said. "It is all over now. The performance can continue."

He turned back to the stage and called back,

"Be off with you, sir. You have now had your say and should retire."

He gave an elegant bow in the direction of the stage, where the man was tramping about clutching his head. His hair fell over his forehead, giving him a look of wild disorder, almost of madness.

"You mock me!" he shrieked. *"But I will rid the world of you!"*

Before everyone's horrified gaze he thrust his hand into his jacket, pulled out a pistol and fired.

There was a loud crack. Then another.

Suddenly everyone was screaming. Lord Thornhill staggered back, clutching his shoulder. The next moment he had toppled over the low divide, straight into Carina's lap.

Her hands flew to her face and she let out a gasp. There was an ugly red stain on the snowy white of his evening shirt.

He began to slide onto the floor and she instinctively put out her arms to save him.

His eyes, which had been closed, opened suddenly. He was looking directly at her.

Carina had the strangest sensation that the world had stopped. She could hear the shouts and screams about her, but they seemed to be coming from a long way away.

The world was suddenly unreal. The only reality was the handsome young man whose head was lying in her lap.

There was blood on his face where the first bullet had grazed his cheekbone before the second bullet caught him in the chest.

He saw her gazing at him, and managed a faint smile.

"Good evening, madam," he said faintly. "My – apologies for – inconveniencing you."

"No – no – " she stammered, too distracted to know what she was saying. "Oh, if only I could help you. Please don't die."

"Certainly not," he murmured. "I would never wish to distress a lady. I think – if a way could be found to stop the bleeding – "

He broke off with a groan.

"Yes, yes," said Carina, looking around her and thinking quickly.

Seizing her reticule, she pulled out a handkerchief. It seemed such a tiny object for such a mighty job, but she screwed it up and thrust it beneath his jacket over the horrible wound.

The man from the next box was leaning over, his face full of horror.

"If you please sir," Carina said, speaking with a calm she was far from feeling, "may I have your handkerchief?"

"I – yes, of course. Well done!"

He handed her a large handkerchief, which Carina pressed into place on the young man's chest, fighting to staunch the flow of blood.

Lord Thornhill was almost unconscious, his eyes fast closing, but still he kept his gaze on her.

"If I live," he whispered, "you will have saved me."

"Oh please don't talk like that," she begged. "You must live. The doctor will be here soon."

"Whatever he does – it is you who has saved me. May I not know your name?"

"Carina," she said.

"Carina. A lovely name. It's Italian, did you know that?"

Tearfully she shook her head.

"In Italian it means 'beloved'. That is how I shall always remember you – my beloved. You are so pretty – I know that one day you will be another man's beloved. But you will always be mine too. I shall never forget you."

"And I shall never forget you," she said, knowing it to be true.

"Kiss me," he whispered.

She gasped at such an outrageous request, but he said,

"It might be my last kiss on earth. I beg you – "

She could not deny him. Dropping her head, she laid her virginal lips briefly on his. For a moment she felt his mouth move against hers. Then he was still.

Horrified she drew back to gaze into his face. Suddenly she became aware of the world again. There were shouts and commotion. The box was filled with people. The doctor had arrived.

The young man was laid out on the floor and the doctor was examining him.

"Come girls," commanded a shaken Miss Ferrars. "We must leave at once."

"Oh no," Carina cried.

"What did you say?"

"I cannot go without knowing if he's dead."

"Do as I tell you and come at once."

Carina's mouth set in a stubbornness that was rare in her.

"No," she said again.

Miss Ferrars gave a little scream of horror. Alice regarded her friend with admiration, but she almost did not recognise her. This was a new Carina, almost a young woman, with strength and determination clearly marked on her brow.

The doctor had found the handkerchiefs.

"Who put these here?"

"I did," Carina faltered.

"Well, you have saved his life."

Carina gave a gasp of joy.

"Then he will live?"

"You have managed to staunch the blood. I see no reason why he should not live now."

"Oh thank you, thank you!"

Carina was swept by violent feeling, too great for her to control. She dropped to her knees, her eyes closed, her lips moving in a prayer of passionate gratitude.

Aghast, Miss Ferrars hauled her to her feet and hurried the two girls out of the box. Carina went in a dream.

All the way home Miss Ferrars was in a flutter. She communicated the terrible deeds to her employers in a voice that suggested the heavens would fall because the two girls had witnessed such things.

Luckily Mr. and Mrs. Grade, although horrified, were people of great common sense and insisted on playing the matter down, forbidding any further mention of it.

There was a brief reference to the shooting in the next day's newspaper, although, to Carina's disappointment, it made no mention of Lord Thornhill's ultimate fate. So she was still left in uncertainty about whether he had lived or died.

On the following day she was sent back to her parents' home in the quiet Worcestershire countryside.

She never told anyone of the words that had passed between her and the young Lord. She never spoke of his kiss or the way he had whispered her name.

But she never forgot him, or the sound of his voice saying, '*Carina – my beloved.*'

Those words would live in her heart forever.

*

1875

The letter from Carina's Aunt Mary arrived just as she was at her lowest point.

It is six months now since your mother died, my dear, and you have lived alone for too long. You are twenty-four and it is time you saw some life. Even now, it isn't too late for you to get married.

Dear Aunt Mary, Carina thought with a smile. She had the tact of an elephant, but she meant to be kind.

And what she said was true. After that one visit to London and the drama of the theatre trip, which now seemed so long ago, nothing remotely exciting had happened to her.

Alice had married at eighteen, not to a man with a title, as her parents had hoped, but to a parson. She now lived in Yorkshire with her husband and four children. Carina had visited them and enjoyed the sight of their happiness, but their lives were placid and uneventful. At last she had been glad to come home.

For years she had been the dutiful daughter in their quiet part of England, playing the piano with her father, who was a considerable musician and was determined to teach her all he knew.

When her father had died of pneumonia, Carina had known that her mother would soon follow him. She no longer had any will to live and had faded into the grave soon after.

Now Carina was alone, twenty-four, an old maid by most standards, yet still beautiful and still clinging to the hope that life might yet hold something for her.

Although not rich, she was comfortably off. She could afford to maintain her household of servants and the horses that were her pride and joy. But loneliness seemed to crush her.

So when Aunt Mary's invitation arrived she hastened to reply, saying that she would join her as soon as she could.

She spent the next day packing all her most attractive clothes and by the following morning she was ready to travel. The carriage took her to the station, the butler and his wife saw her off and she was on her way. To an adventure, she hoped.

As Carina sat in the train, she considered the immediate future.

Her aunt lived in the country in Sussex, but sufficiently close to a small town to make Carina view the prospect with pleasure.

'It is a pity Aunt Mary doesn't live in London,' she thought. 'That would be really exciting. If I had been in London, I might have had several proposals of marriage by now.'

When she was at school, the girls had always been gossiping about the men they had danced with when they were at home for the holidays.

If they had been a success, they boasted of it to their friends the following term.

"He sent me flowers every day," claimed one girl, whose name was Sally. "Then he tried to kiss me. But I remembered my mother said that if I allowed a man to kiss me, I would seem cheap and rather improper, so I said 'no'."

"You might have agreed just for once," said another girl who was called Jane.

The others laughed, and Sally said,

"Mama says that if you let a man kiss you, he no longer respects you and he would never ask you to marry him."

That caused a great deal of discussion.

Some girls said they had been kissed and it was disappointing.

Others said their mothers had been very angry because they had allowed themselves to be kissed, and they had been told that if it happened again they would not be allowed to go to any balls.

"I think," said another girl called Helen, "that if you want him to propose marriage, you should be very coy and make it clear that you have never been kissed until that moment."

"Why should we do that?" Carina asked.

"Because a man wants to marry a girl who loves him more than anyone else," was the reply. "So he doesn't want to think you have kissed any other man."

"What about you, Carina?" Jane asked. "Have you ever been kissed?"

"I – no – not exactly."

The others clamoured to know what 'not exactly' meant. But Carina refused to say any more.

She was seventeen. The strange, dramatic kiss she had received from the young man who might have been dying, lived in her memory like a rose preserved between the pages of a book. But she knew it was not what the girls meant and she was determined to keep silent about it.

"No, I have never been kissed," she said firmly.

But she could not help wondering what the real thing would be like. Would it be as romantic and exciting as in her dreams? She wondered how she would feel as the man's arms closed around her and his lips touched hers.

Carina remembered that conversation as she sat in the train taking her to her aunt's home.

'I am twenty-four,' she told herself, 'and I've never been kissed – except for that one strange occasion, which is hardly the same thing – and no man has ever proposed marriage to me. I suppose most of the girls I was with at school would laugh and say I am a failure.'

She sighed as she continued,

'But it's not my fault that I never had the chance of any of these things happening.'

At last she reached her destination. She jumped out and walked towards the end of the train where the men were unloading the luggage including her own.

Suddenly she saw her aunt hurrying towards her at the far end of the platform.

With a cry of joy Carina ran towards her and kissed her affectionately.

"Forgive me for being late," her aunt said. "I was held up at the last moment by a message from some friends, who I will tell you all about, but let us get your luggage onto the carriage first."

When it was all loaded and they were driving off, Aunt Mary said,

"It is lovely to see you, dear, and how pretty you are. I had forgotten that you are as lovely as your mother was when she was your age, and every man who met her fell in love with her."

Carina laughed.

"Oh, do tell me about it," she urged. "Mama was always rather shy about discussing what a success she was. But several people have told me she was the prettiest girl at every ball and every man laid his heart at her feet."

Aunt Mary chuckled

"That is true, I can assure you," she replied. "As you know, I was two years older than your mother, but I always hoped that one day I would be as popular as she was. I never managed it, but I am sure that you will."

Carina smiled and said,

"It is difficult to be a success on your own. As you know we live in a very lonely part of Worcestershire and since Mama died I have hardly seen anyone."

"What you are really saying," her aunt replied, "is that there are too few men to make that part of the world exciting."

"Yes, I suppose I am."

"Things are certainly going to be different while you are staying with me," Aunt Mary said. "But there will be a slight delay. I find I must rush off suddenly to see my sister-in-law, who has had a nasty riding accident.

"I am afraid, dearest, that I will have to leave tomorrow and be away for several nights. I am so sorry this should happen just when you have come to stay with me."

"I quite understand," Carina replied, swallowing her disappointment. "Of course if you had told me not to come, I would have waited until your return."

"I thought of that," her aunt said, "but everything is arranged, and I will not be away for long."

"Don't worry," Carina said. "It will be so exciting to look at your house and explore the garden."

But as she spoke she recalled that she had come here hoping for a great deal more than that.

By now they had left the station behind and were out in the country. Soon they arrived at her aunt's house, a comfortable stone mansion set in extensive grounds.

Carina was thrilled to find it even larger and prettier than she had expected. Everything in it was costly and elegant. Footmen carried her luggage to her room and a maid was appointed to take care of her.

Over dinner that evening she thought the food was the most delicious she had ever tasted.

"As soon as I get back, we will make plans," Aunt Mary said. "There are a great number of people around here who I want you to meet."

"That would be wonderful," Carina sighed. "I have always longed for an exciting social life."

"It is what you should have enjoyed a long time ago," her aunt replied. "I always thought my sister and her husband were mad burying themselves alive, as it were, in

13

that boring part of Worcestershire."

"But they were very happy," Carina said wistfully, thinking of her parents.

"I know. That is why I didn't worry about them. But I should have worried more about you. A girl so lovely has been simply wasted in that place. Never mind. It's never too late. There are plenty of men who will run after you now."

"Do you have any really thrilling neighbours?"

"Hmm! Well, I suppose some people would call the Duke of Westbury thrilling, but in my view he is a rather disreputable character."

"Really?" Carina asked, her eyes wide.

She had never met a disreputable man, except for Lord Thornhill. He had been in and out of her life so quickly that she had never learned much about him, although she supposed he must have been shocking for a man to have shot him from the stage.

"Oh, I would like to meet the Duke," she said.

"That is a most improper observation, miss! He gives receptions at the castle and I dare say we will be invited. Courtesy will oblige us to accept, but no more. He is not a suitable man for you to know."

"But why?"

"I have told you, he is a disreputable character."

"But what does that mean?"

"I haven't time to go into it now," her aunt said hastily. "In time you will meet him, say hello politely and that will be that."

"Oh Aunt, surely you can tell me something more about him?"

"In his youth he fought duels."

"Goodness! But duels have been against the law for a

long time. He must be absolutely ancient."

"He is in his thirties."

"You mean he fought duels against the law? How very brave he must be!"

"This is a disgraceful conversation. He is not a man of good character and would not be received in polite society, but he is thick as thieves with the Prince of Wales."

"Is not the Prince of Wales a man of good character?"

"It's time we were going to bed. We'll talk more when I return."

"Yes, Aunt," Carina said.

Her voice was meek, but inwardly she thought this was the most exciting conversation she had ever had.

The Duke was a man of bad character, 'thick as thieves' with the Prince of Wales, also hopefully a man of bad character.

How thrilling life was proving already!

CHAPTER TWO

Aunt Mary set off early in the morning and told Carina to treat the house as her own.

As soon as she was alone, she began to explore the garden.

She loved gardens and thought that her aunt's house, which went back to medieval times, boasted a garden which was almost a dream.

'It is entrancing,' she told herself, as she stopped beside a very large tree and saw, as she looked up, that there were nests in it.

After the garden she explored the fields which held her aunt's horses. They were as fine, if not finer than her own. She spent a long time admiring them.

She had reached the end of the field and was looking over the ancient brick wall into the road beyond.

It was then that she saw a horse-drawn van, coming down the road past the ornamental gates. It was the kind of van which transported logs and it was travelling at a reckless speed.

There was a sharp turn at the end of the road, and Carina realised suddenly that the van was going too fast to take it successfully. The next moment there was a loud crash and a scream, followed by two male voices shouting.

'Oh heavens, there's been an accident,' she thought as

she ran across the field to the gate.

Dashing through it, she ran to the corner, and as soon as she turned she could see what had happened.

The van had crashed into a large carriage, drawn by two horses, and driven it into a ditch.

The horses were apparently unhurt but the carriage itself was damaged.

Two men were helping a smartly dressed young woman, with a badly bleeding hand, to leave the carriage and sit down, leaning against the wall.

"Can I help you?" Carina enquired. "I live in that house over there. Perhaps you had better bring her in and we can send for a doctor."

One of the men rose to face Carina. He was middle-aged, well-dressed, but with a slightly rakish air that she could not quite define.

"You are very kind, madam," he said.

Several other carriages had now caught up with them and people were jumping down and hurrying over. Most of them, Carina noticed, seemed to be young and very pretty women.

"Are you all together?" she asked.

"We are indeed, madam," said the man, sweeping off his hat with a little flourish. "Allow me to introduce myself. I am Bertram Hentege, at your service.

"We are a company of performers, very much in demand, if I may say so, and on our way to a most prestigious engagement."

"*Bertie!*" yelled a man from just behind him. "Can't all that wait until later?"

"Oh dear, what am I thinking of?" Bertie replied guiltily. "Yes, of course. I was merely explaining that we are all together – "

"Then you had better all come to the house," Carina said. "I will show you the way."

Several of them helped the injured woman into another carriage. Some of the men were tending the horses, while others were having a lively argument with the van driver who had caused the accident.

Eventually he drove off, hurling abuse over his shoulder.

"Up there," Carina told Bertie, pointing to the house. "I'll go on ahead to warn them."

Taking a short cut, she was able to reach the house first and speak to Jennings, the butler. He nodded when he heard about the van.

"It's them from the forest," he said. "They always drive too fast."

"I would like the injured woman to rest in one of the bedrooms until the doctor comes."

The next half hour was taken up with practical arrangements. The carriages arrived at the house and the young woman was taken upstairs, while a footman was despatched for the doctor.

Carina went up to see that the woman was made as comfortable as possible. She was clearly in pain, but she smiled bravely and was able to drink some tea.

After a few minutes Bertie came in. Her eyes flew to his face and she said in a conscience stricken voice,

"I am so sorry, Bertie."

"Don't worry about it now, my dear," he said kindly. "We'll think of something."

Carina left them together and went down to the sitting room where the rest of the party had been taken.

There were three men and three women all of whom were dressed in a slightly extravagant manner, which reminded her that they were performers.

When Carina entered the room, the men who had been sitting down, rose to their feet.

"Good afternoon," she said. "I am Miss Carina Denton."

To her relief Bertie entered almost at once, and said,

"My dear young lady, what can I say? A thousand thanks for your kindness."

He then disconcerted her by seizing her hand and kissing it with a theatrical flourish.

"Please," she said, "it was nothing."

"Nothing. It was *everything!*" He threw his arms wide in a gesture that seemed meant to encompass the entire world.

"But for you," he went on, "we would have been destitute, abandoned to our wretched fate, miserable outcasts, condemned to wander the land in search of succour – "

"Bertie!" one of the girls chided him in a voice that mixed exasperation and fondness equally.

He came down to earth, saying in a normal tone,

"I can only hope that the doctor will be able to treat Melanie's arm."

"It seemed bad as it was bleeding so much," one of the men pointed out.

"I know," Bertie said gravely. "The poor girl's in a terrible state. I reassured her as best I could, but if she cannot perform, well – "

He gave a despairing shrug.

"Do you mean that we won't be able to perform tonight?" one of the girls asked.

"How can we, if Melanie cannot play?" Bertie replied

almost angrily.

Then he closed his fists and held them above his head.

"Why should this happen to me," he cried, "just at the moment when His Grace has invited us to entertain his friends?"

"His Grace?" Carina asked.

"The Duke of Westbury," Bertie told her. "We are due at his house in the next hour or so."

"Are you giving him a special performance?" she asked, thrilled.

"A special command performance," Bertie said impressively. "You may have heard of *Bertie's Beauties*."

He said the last words as though announcing the Queen. Clearly Carina was expected to be struck dumb with amazement.

But she shook her head.

"Not heard of us?" Bertie asked, aghast. "But we regularly take London by storm."

"I haven't been to London for a long time," she told him.

"Well, we are a huge attraction. His Grace said that we were just what he wanted to perform for his friends tonight and tomorrow night."

He buried his face in his hands and demanded in throbbing accents,

"How could we imagine such a tragedy? To have such an accident only a mile from Westbury Castle!"

Carina was intrigued.

"Do tell me what you do?" she asked.

"We sing, we dance and we are the best after-dinner entertainment in the whole of London," Bertie declared grandiloquently.

She could not help smiling. Boastful though he might me, there was something about him that she could not help liking.

"I would love to see you perform," she said.

"I would love you to do so," he retorted. "But it seems we'll not be able to go on tonight."

"Why not?" Carina asked.

Before he could answer Jennings came in.

"You are in luck," he said. "My man stopped the doctor just a short distance away and brought him straight here."

Bertie whirled and immediately made for the door. Carina heard him talking nineteen to the dozen all the way up the stairs.

"Please forgive Bertie's rather strange manners," said a dark haired girl. "He is the kindest soul in the world really, but he lives and breathes performing and he somehow expects everyone to understand that."

"Do tell me who you are and what you do?" Carina asked again.

"I am Julia. We sing and we dance and – " her voice became an imitation of Bertie's, "we are undoubtedly the most successful turn in the whole of London."

The others laughed as she became herself again.

"That's right," said a very handsome young man with curly hair. "They say people even come from the continent to see us. I am James, by the way. This is Helen, this is Belinda, and these fellows here are Anthony and Samson."

Carina shook hands with everyone.

Then Helen said,

"But if Melanie's not fit to perform, what shall we do?"

"Why is she so vital?" Carina asked.

"Because she plays the piano," Anthony replied. "If there's no music we can't dance or sing and then nobody can see *Bertie's Beauties*."

They all laughed at the way Anthony had spoken.

"Why is it so important to perform for the Duke?" Carina asked.

"Well, first because he is a Duke," Anthony replied. "Secondly, because what he does is copied by a great number of people who admire him, and Bertie is absolutely certain that if we are a success at his house, we will be asked to almost every ancestral house in the country, especially when it's winter and the host and his guests have been hunting all day."

He laughed as he added,

"What they need in the evening is *Bertie's Beauties* to cheer them up."

Carina was fascinated and she wanted to know more.

But while the girls began to tell her about their performances, they heard Bertie's voice outside and there was a sudden silence.

All eyes were on him as he walked in and threw himself down on the sofa in an attitude of despair.

"What has happened?" Samson asked.

"Need you ask?" Bertie replied. "Melanie's hand is badly cut. If she's careful with it, it should be better in three or four days, but not before."

There was a cry from everyone.

Then Anthony asked,

"Are you quite certain we cannot perform tonight?"

"How can we perform without a pianist?" Bertie asked despondently. "We will have to tell His Grace that we've had an accident, and just pray that one day he'll ask us again."

He did not sound hopeful.

"Surely one of us can play the piano?" Julia said.

They all exchanged glances, but there was silence. Nobody volunteered.

Carina drew in her breath, startled by the daring idea that had come into her mind. It was unthinkable.

And yet –

Bertie looked like an overgrown baby, who might burst into tears at any moment.

Out of sight, Carina clenched her fists. It was now or never.

"Perhaps I can play for you," she suggested tentatively.

Everyone stared at her.

Then Bertie spoke in a dazed voice.

"Are you a good pianist?"

"I won several prizes when I was at school," Carina told him. "I have practiced a great deal lately because I've been alone. In fact, I am sure I can read any music you want."

Bertie gave a cry and jumped to his feet.

"You are a pianist! You are a *pianist!*" he exclaimed. "Where is the piano in this house?"

"In the room next door," Carina said.

"Wait here," Bertie called, dashing out of the house.

He was back in a moment with a case that he had snatched from one of the carriages. Carina had already gone to the next room and opened the lid of the piano.

Bertie hurried in, took out some sheets of music, and handed them to her, staring at her imploringly.

"You are making me nervous," she said. "I can only

hope that I can play as well as Melanie."

"Try! Try!" Bertie begged.

Carina sat down at the piano.

She ran her fingers over the keys just to be sure that the piano was in tune. Then she looked at the music Bertie had put in front of her.

Suddenly she realised it was not at all difficult. She had played much harder music in the past.

She began to play. In a few seconds she knew she had the measure of this music. She speeded up, dashing off a bravura passage in dazzling time and finishing with a flourish.

Everyone was wreathed in smiles, clapping eagerly.

"Brilliant! Absolutely brilliant!"

Bertie was dancing with excitement.

"You are an angel sent from heaven to rescue us when I thought there was no hope left," he cried.

"Are you quite certain I can do what you want?" Carina asked.

"All I want you to do is to play as you did just now," Bertie told her. "I gave you the most difficult music, in order to test you. The rest is much easier."

Tact prevented Carina from saying that Bertie's notion of 'difficult music' was rather elementary. All that mattered was that she was up to the task.

"You are wonderful," he exclaimed. "Thanks to you, we are going to be a great success."

"So what happens now?" Carina wanted to know.

"We have to be at the castle by tonight," Bertie said. "So go and pack your things and make sure you bring your most beautiful clothes. You will be looked at as well as heard."

"It sounds so thrilling," Carina said excitedly. "I just hope I don't let you down."

"You will be the making of us," Bertie insisted. "The Duke is very demanding. He orders the best, pays for the best and expects the best and that is what we are going to give him."

"If His Grace doesn't appreciate the prettiest pianist in the business," said Anthony, "then he is an ungrateful dog."

Carina smiled. Then she blushed.

"Now you are making me feel embarrassed," she said. "So I will hurry up and get my clothes ready. But please do not expect too much as it is something I have never done before."

"You can take it from me," James said, "you will want to do it again and again. You'll find the applause irresistible, as we all do."

Everyone laughed at that.

"I'll send the butler to you with refreshments while I get my things together," Carina said calmly. "Perhaps one of the girls will come with me and tell me what to bring."

"I'll come," Julia offered.

As they walked upstairs she said,

"I really think poor old Bertie would have cried if he couldn't perform tonight. He was so delighted to be invited to Westbury Towers, which is supposed to be almost a palace. Have you ever been inside?"

"Oh no, I don't live here normally" Carina replied. "I know nothing about the Duke, except that my aunt says he's disreputable. But I am not sure why."

"He's famous for it," Julia said knowingly.

"Famous for what?"

"Being disreputable. Apparently his house is full of

'goings on'."

"What kind of goings on?" Carina asked, breathlessly.

"You know – *goings on.* The sort nobody knows about."

"But if nobody knows about them, how does anyone know they are going on?"

"Because he is notorious in London," Julia said unanswerably. "He is known for his parties, because he always has something unusual and different to entertain his guests."

"So tonight that's *Bertie's Beauties*?" Carina asked curiously.

Julia smiled.

"We normally perform at the Globe Theatre, which is known as being the most popular place with men. Most women think it rather fast and I suppose at times slightly vulgar. So it is men like the Duke who patronise us."

They had reached Carina's room. She opened her wardrobes, and Julia's eyes opened wide at some of her dresses.

"Oh yes, you will do very well," she exclaimed. "A real *Bertie's Beauty*. The men will certainly admire you."

"But – surely all the guests won't be men?" Carina asked. She was beginning to wonder what she was getting herself into.

"I wouldn't be surprised," Julia said airily. "If there are any female guests they'll probably be actresses or ladies who are not accepted by the *Beau Monde.*"

Carina drew in her breath.

She realised now that she should not go to such parties.

She had heard of them taking place when she was at school but they were whispered about from one girl to another.

It was not that they themselves had attended such parties, but their brothers had done so and talked about them when they were at home.

'I shouldn't really be doing this,' she thought guiltily.

Julia was studying Carina's clothes, choosing those with the lowest necklines. Carina realised that they would naturally wear gowns that were lower and more revealing than anything to be seen in polite society.

So often she had heard people say,

"Oh, she is only an actress."

Or there would be a note in someone's voice as they spoke of a gentleman pursuing a certain kind of woman that would suggest the woman was fast and not accepted by those who lived in Society.

And now she would be entering the world of women who were 'not quite acceptable'.

She tried to feel shocked, but she could not hide from herself that she was curious and fascinated.

'I am not going to worry about it,' she told herself firmly. 'It won't hurt me to spend a couple of nights under the Duke's roof. He'll think I am one of *Bertie's Beauties* and no one need ever know who I actually am.

'This is an adventure, and I am going to enjoy every moment of it."

*

Lord Bruno Heydock's roar of laughter sounded like a bull. He was bellowing now at some sally from one of his fellow guests. It had been a vulgar joke, which was how Lord Bruno liked them.

"Dashed fine place you've got here, Westbury," he said, making a gesture that was meant to take in the whole castle.

The Duke of Westbury, a tall elegant figure, shrugged.

"It suffices," he said in a bored voice.

"Dammit man, you've got the best of everything. The best horses, the best servants, the best brandy."

As he said this, he stared into the bottom of his empty glass. The Duke made a discreet signal to a nearby footman, who immediately approached, bearing a fresh decanter of brandy.

With his glass full again, Lord Bruno was happy.

"If you drink too much now you won't be awake when Westbury springs his surprise on us this evening," said Viscount Manton.

"It's not a surprise," the Duke observed. "I have merely hired a very fine troupe of entertainers called *Bertie's Beauties.*"

"Ah, now that's more like it," Lord Bruno growled. "Pretty girls and lots of them."

Some more men entered, having come straight from the stables. They had been riding hard and were ready to eat, drink and be entertained.

"Tell us about *Bertie's Beauties,*" Lord Bruno insisted.

"Wait and all will be revealed," the Duke replied mysteriously.

He seemed completely at his ease, lounging on a chair in his elegant, luxurious library, the very picture of the wealthy country gentleman, with nothing to do but enjoy the heartier pleasures of the flesh.

But Viscount Manton, who was his special friend, was alert to a touch of weariness in the Duke, who took no further part in the conversation, but stayed as he was, one long leg hooked over the arm of his chair.

His dark hair was tousled from an energetic ride and one lock fell over his forehead. The Duke's face was not merely handsome but striking, vivid and turbulent, the eyes with a touch of fierceness.

His mouth was heavily sensual, especially now that he was relaxed. His nose was long and straight, his chin stubborn.

What saved his face from being too perfect was a scar on one cheekbone from the graze of a bullet. The Viscount had heard the rumours of how, as a much younger man, his friend had been shot by an outraged husband, during a theatrical performance. Some people said he had nearly died.

The Duke himself never spoke of the matter nor allowed it to be mentioned. And his very silence only contributed to the stories that swirled about him. He was said to be a bad man, a libertine, given over to every form of excess.

The Duke never contradicted the tales. Either it suited him to be thought kin to the devil, or he cared nothing for anyone's opinion. The Viscount suspected it was a little of both.

When the others had moved away he asked gently,

"What's up, old fellow?"

The Duke shrugged.

"I don't know – nothing."

"Aren't you enjoying the weekend party?"

"Of course. Excessively! It's just that – I can't explain – don't you ever get weary of climbing round and round on the same old treadmill."

"A treadmill of pleasure," the Viscount reminded him.

"True. But after a while it loses its savour and you start to see how pointless it all is."

"I have never heard you say such a thing before," the Viscount said, startled. "It's just as Bruno said – "

"Bruno's an insensitive oaf," the Duke interrupted testily.

"True, but he was right this time. You've got everything a man could want, a great title, land, this house, the best wine, the best horses, your pick of every woman you meet – "

"But the kind of woman who is there for the picking – the kind we will meet today, for instance – palls after a while," the Duke observed moodily.

"You've got first choice of the others too," the Viscount pointed out. "You cannot stay single forever. It is time you married and set up your nursery and everyone knows it if you don't."

"Oh, I know it well enough. I am reminded every time I meet a respectable woman and feel the world's eyes on me, wondering if this will be the one to make me yield. Dammit, just how bad does my reputation have to be to scare off the match-making Mamas?"

"A lot worse than it is," his friend observed wryly. "I don't know what you would have to do to obscure the glory of a ducal coronet and the friendship of royalty. Murder perhaps."

The Duke gave a harsh laugh.

"Exactly. The respectable women are no better than the other kind. They are every bit as calculating. It's just that they are calculating something different. Their ostentatious 'virtue' is no more than the price of becoming a Duchess.

"I prefer the kind of girls who join *Bertie's Beauties*. They don't pretend to be something they're not and the transaction is honestly carried out."

"That's a damned cynical thing to say!"

"I am a cynical man. I have reason to be."

"So according to you the female world is divided into these two kinds. And there is nothing in between?"

"Oh, I suppose there must be women somewhere who are not for sale in either one way or the other. True women, with honest hearts, incapable of deception."

"But you've never met one, I suppose?"

"No – that is, she wasn't exactly a woman, just a girl."

"This sounds intriguing. Tell me about her."

But the Duke shook his head.

"No, I can't do that. In a sense she doesn't even exist. It was long ago and she was very young. When she grew up she probably turned out just like all the others."

"Maybe not. Maybe she is still perfect and you will meet your ideal again, somewhere along the way."

But at that the Duke made a sound of disgust.

"My ideal! What a sentimental fool you make me sound! Wise men don't have ideals, because sooner or later all ideals get smashed."

For a moment he touched the scar on his cheek.

Then he snatched his hand away, as though catching himself up in some weakness.

He leapt to his feet, seizing the brandy decanter.

"Let's join the others," he said harshly. "Come on, Manton, it's time to get ready for the party. We're going to have the night of our lives."

CHAPTER THREE

It was time for Carina and the troupe to leave. She had put on one of her best dresses and added a very pretty hat.

When she went downstairs, Bertie took one look at her and clapped his hands.

"Magnificent!" he exclaimed. "You are a true *Bertie's Beauty*."

Carina blushed.

"I don't think you should say that," she said. "It sounds – not quite proper."

"Nonsense, you are a lovely girl. You shouldn't be ashamed that men admire you."

There was something so engagingly innocent about him that it was impossible to take offence. After a moment she laughed and he joined her.

"You don't mind if I say how talented you are?" he asked. "How could I have been so lucky as to have found you?"

"I hope you will still say that after the performance," Carina retorted with spirit.

Bertie roared with laughter.

"Wit as well as beauty!" he declared with a theatrical flourish.

Melanie was still asleep. Carina had already told the housekeeper to explain what had happened when she woke, and take the best possible care of her. Now she was free to let Bertie lead her out to the carriage.

"By the way," he said, "I know you won't want the Duke to know your real name, and I would like you to take the name of a flower."

"A flower?" Carina questioned.

"All the girls have chosen flowers as their stage names. Julia is Pansy, Helen is Rose, Belinda is Daisy, Melanie is Rosetta. So choose a flower that you like, and that will be your stage name."

"What a lovely idea. I must think about it for a while"

After they had travelled a few miles she said,

"Tell me some more about the Duke. Have you ever actually met him?"

"Oh yes. I was employed as a college servant when he was at Oxford University. Many's the time I helped to put him to bed."

"Oh! You mean when he was – ?"

"The worse for wear," Bertie supplied. "All students go a little wild, although I must admit that he was wilder than most. He was sent down a couple of times and it would have been more if I hadn't covered up for him."

Carina's lips twitched.

"I am sure he was very grateful to you?"

"He was. Generous too, I have to admit. In fact, when he left Oxford he asked me to come and work for him. He said he knew he was dissipated and he meant to go on being dissipated, and he'd feel easier if I was watching over him."

"But you didn't accept?"

"I just wanted to get back to my life in the theatre. I used to be an actor, you know. A real actor, Shakespeare and all that. I was famous for my *Macbeth*."

He assumed a melodramatic air, holding up his hand

and gazing fixedly at it to declaim,

"Is this a dagger I see before me?"

"Mind you," he said, relapsing into a normal voice, "I was chiefly famous because I dropped the dagger."

Carina chuckled.

"I was never much use as a tragedian," he went on. "More of a clown really and I could sing all the songs."

He began to sing.

"When I was but a little tiny boy,
With a heigh-ho, the wind and the rain."

"Feste from *Twelfth Night,"* Carina said at once.

"That's right. You know Shakespeare. Wonderful."

"Well, I do know that play. I saw it performed in London once."

Her voice trailed away as she recalled that night and the vivid young man lying in her arms, perhaps bleeding to death. The doctor had said he ought to live, but she would never really know.

"I thought that was such a sad song," she told Bertie now. "The way poor Feste kept singing, *'The rain it raineth every day.'* It made you feel that he was always going to be sad."

"That is how I tried to play it," Bertie said triumphantly. "The anguish beneath the clown's smile."

"But why did you leave the stage if you loved it so much?"

"It left me," Bertie said with a melancholy sigh. "There wasn't enough work, so I took any job I could get, which is how I became a college servant.

"I worked hard, saved all the tips and eventually had enough to think of starting again. I told the Duke all this when I turned his job down, and he laughed and gave me two hundred pounds to help me get started."

"So the Duke is really behind *Bertie's Beauties*?" Carina asked.

"In a way, yes, although *Berties' Beauties* were still in the future then. I teamed up with a lady, singing duets at the piano.

"We were doing really well. I was even thinking of asking her to make our partnership permanent in every sense. But she ran off with a trombone player. Heigh ho! It certainly rained that day."

"Poor Bertie," Carina said, but she could not help smiling.

"I had to find someone else. I ended up with twins. They weren't brilliant performers but they were absolutely identical and they did everything in perfect unison."

"Everything?" Carina asked before she could control her unruly tongue.

"So they informed me," Bertie said, not meeting her eye. Anyway, the audience loved them. I employed some more artistes, and that is how the act was born.

"Of course I had to engage some men as well, so that they could dance and sing romantic duets together. But it's my gorgeous girls the public comes to see."

"And you have stayed in touch with the Duke?" Carina asked.

"He's seen the show in London a couple of times, but this is the first time he has invited us to his home. Between you and me, the private house circuit is very profitable."

"More than the theatre? Why?"

But this question caused Bertie to become flustered. He had, he realised, been more forth-coming than he had intended. Carina was a respectable girl and would not understand nor approve of the relationships that could grow up between his ladies and his customers.

One of his girls had actually married into the peerage, although that was rare. Most of them had to be content with diamonds.

To his great relief Carina had turned her attention to the passing scenery.

When they came to some high, ornamental gates she knew they had reached the Duke's home.

Two men pulled the gates wide open for the carriages to pass through.

"Don't forget to tell me what flower name you want to take," Bertie reminded her.

"Oh, yes. I think I'd like to be called Iris."

"Lovely. Nice and musical! And you are so pretty, I think a number of His Grace's guests will be calling you their favourite flower."

When she had her first glimpse of the Duke's castle, Carina gave a cry of delight.

"It is so beautiful! Really beautiful!" she exclaimed.

The castle was certainly impressive, rearing up, silhouetted against the sky, with a flag flying on the top of the tower.

The windows were glinting in the sunshine and she thought the castle and its surroundings might have come straight from a picture book or, better still, a fairy story.

'This is an adventure I did not expect,' she thought. 'I will certainly have a story to tell when I leave.'

But then she wondered to whom she could possibly tell this story. Who was there who would not be shocked by it?

They drew up at a side door. There was a servant to welcome them and men to carry the luggage upstairs to the bedrooms they had been allocated.

As soon as they arrived refreshments were brought to

each individual bedroom.

'We are obviously not to meet the Duke and his friends,' she thought, 'until we are dressed up and ready to perform. I suppose he doesn't think we are good enough to mix with his important guests.'

A maid unpacked her dresses and hung them up. As Carina was considering which one to wear, there was a knock at her door. It was Bertie.

"I have brought you something that may make you feel better about appearing," he said.

To her delight he held up a mask made of crimson lace and satin. When in position it covered the upper part of her face.

"Oh, I like this," she cried. "It is so pretty, and modest."

"I have been looking at where we will be performing tonight," he said. "Would you like to come and check the piano?"

"I would love to. I need to try the piano while I am wearing this mask, to make sure that I can see properly."

Together they found the music room. When Carina saw it, she gave a little cry of admiration.

At one end was a raised platform, on which stood a grand piano. Behind it were several floor length windows. There were no lights on and the curtains were drawn, excluding the day, so that the room was dim and shadowy.

There were flowers at the base of the platform as well as at either side of the seats where the guests would be sitting.

"The flowers are so lovely!" Carina exclaimed.

"I thought you'd admire them," Bertie replied. "I think the Duke was remembering that all my female performers are named after flowers. You must not forget that you are, too."

"Now sit down and try the piano. Is there enough light for you to see?"

"Yes, I don't need any more. I like this shadowy atmosphere".

Again Carina found the music easy and luckily the mask did not impede her view. She looked up at Bertie, and found him regarding her with a smile on his face of such heavenly satisfaction that she could not help laughing.

Suddenly there was a small interruption. One of the girls came hurrying in, begging Bertie to come upstairs and sort out a little problem.

"You go," Carina told him. "I want to get the feel of the piano."

As soon as he had gone she plunged into music that was more difficult. It was a magnificent instrument, the best she had ever played and she wanted the pleasure of practising on it as long as possible.

She could not have said exactly when she became aware that somebody was watching her. It was as though the man had always been there, standing very still.

It was his very stillness that alerted her. He was in the shadows of the doorway, almost as though he had materialised from them. He stayed there, motionless, as though he could not tear his eyes away from her.

Carina was playing Chopin, a soft and dreamy piece, full of longing and melancholy. Only as it drew to a close did he start to move towards her.

"That was beautiful," he said quietly.

He was somewhere in his thirties, she guessed, tall, powerful, with dark hair. More than that she could not see in the dim light.

"Thank you," she said.

"Play something else."

The words were a command but strangely they sounded more like a plea. Carina played more Chopin, choosing another piece that was full of sorrow. As she played he moved slowly across the floor until he was close to her.

The last note died away into the silence.

"Shall I play something else?" she asked, speaking softly so as not to break the spell.

"No, that was perfect," he said. "The saddest music I ever heard."

"When Chopin wrote it, he said it was supposed to represent someone looking at an old house where he had once been very happy," Carina told him.

"Yes," he replied at once. "That's exactly it. Happiness gone forever. Only emptiness and desolation left."

Something in his voice impelled her to ask,

"Is that what happened to your happiness?"

"No. It's hard to explain. I never had that much happiness, only pleasure which is not the same thing. And what I had was never taken away from me. It just – soured somehow, and became meaningless."

"But that is sadder than anything," Carina said. "To have lost happiness without having really known it."

He moved nearer.

"What a curious thing to say!" he said.

Carina smiled up at him.

Then the smile froze on her lips.

She blinked and looked again, sure that she must have made a mistake.

But there was no mistake.

It was Lord Thornhill.

He was older, slightly heavier and his face had an added harshness. But she recognised the dark, brilliant eyes with their turbulent expression.

And there was the scar on his cheek where the bullet had grazed it.

There was no doubt about it. This was the young man from long ago, who had nearly died in her arms.

Carina was about to give a cry of pleasure and tell him who she was, but she choked it back.

She was here as an actress, the kind of woman with whom a man would think liberties could be taken, because she was not truly respectable.

His words from that night came back to her.

"That is how I shall always remember you – my beloved."

He had promised to keep her as a sacred, cherished memory and perhaps he had. If so, she could not bear to ruin that memory now.

He did not show any sign of recognition and she guessed that the mask covered enough of her face to protect her.

"What is your name?" he asked.

"Iris."

"Don't you have another name?"

She shook her head.

"Why are you wearing a mask? Ah, I know. You must be one of the entertainers. Bertie always calls them after flowers. I knew there must be some reason why I had never seen you before?"

"Perhaps you have," she mused. It was a reckless thing to say, but she could not resist venturing, just a little.

"No, I should know you at once. The other girls may

call themselves beauties, but you really are one."

"You cannot possibly know that."

"I can see your mouth, and it's a lovely mouth. Whether it's still or smiling, it's the most kissable mouth I have ever seen."

No man had ever said such a thing to her before, and she felt a moment of shock. But it was all right, she thought, as long as her true identity was concealed. She could even allow herself a moment of guilty enjoyment.

"You are too kind, sir," she said, running her hands over the keys again.

"Then why won't you look at me?"

"I can hear you without looking at you."

"Now you're playing games. You know that as soon as you look up, I shall kiss you."

"You might try."

"Are you saying that you wouldn't let me?"

She knew that at this point she should throw a fit of maidenly vapours and flee him. Instead she gave him a sideways glance and a mysterious smile, saying,

"I haven't yet made up my mind. You might not suit me at all."

"You are very unjust. Without knowing anything about me, you decide against me."

"Oh, I know something about you. I know that you're a bad man."

"Where the devil did you get that idea?"

"Because you're a guest of the Duke, and everyone knows that *he's* a bad man."

He raised one eyebrow in wry hilarity.

"Now, this I must hear. Exactly what is His Grace guilty of?"

"He has a shocking reputation," Carina said carefully. "Why?"

"Because – because of what happens in this castle," she said, wishing she had never started this. "Orgies and – and goings on."

"So you think I must be equally guilty? Well, I admit that my being here might bear that interpretation. As you say, the Duke is a desperate character, steeped in villainy. Luckily for him, his worst excesses have never yet become known."

"Really?" she asked, gazing at him wide-eyed.

"You should beware. When you look at me like that, I am tempted to kiss you whether you like it or not. Mind you – I think you *would* like it, when it does happen."

"We shall never know," she replied primly.

He laughed and the sound sent a thrill scurrying through her.

"Oh, I think we will, eventually. Something tells me that you and I are destined to kiss – and kiss again. And I think, in the end, I could make you enjoy it. Don't you think I could?"

Carina almost gasped at the feeling of excitement that pervaded her at these shocking words. He was only talking to her, not even touching her, but he seemed to be weaving spells all around her.

She forced herself to speak calmly.

"I have no opinion on the matter."

He laughed again, a deep attractive sound that was almost her undoing.

"There's only one way to find out," he said.

She was assailed by a temptation to let him kiss her, but she forced herself to be strong. To yield would be to confirm his belief that she was a loose woman, there for the taking.

"I think perhaps we had better not find out," she said.

"The devil you do!"

"You should not invoke the devil to help you," she told him. "He cannot tempt me, any more than you can."

There was pride in her refusal. But also, if she was honest with herself, there was the desire to keep him guessing.

She knew she had succeeded when he regarded her with his head on one side and an expression of curiosity in his eyes.

"Let me assure you, pretty lady, I am quite capable of tempting a woman on my own merits without invoking help from the devil."

"Perhaps," she riposted lightly. "Some women."

"But not you, eh?"

"But not me."

"So it will be a duel between us? Dashed if I ever enjoyed the prospect more."

She did not answer, but her fingers drifted over the keys, playing softly.

When he saw that he could not lure her into a reply he said,

"Of course, you might have misjudged me. The Duke is undoubtedly a villain, but I might be trying to reclaim him. Have you thought of that?"

"No, and I don't believe it."

His eyes gleamed.

"You think I am as bad as he?"

"What I think is that you are making fun of me."

He laughed out loud.

"But my dear girl, how can I help it? Your way of

looking at the world is enchanting. I will plead guilty to attending the Duke's bachelor parties and enjoying some amusements that would shock polite society.

"But permit me to point out that, as a musical performer, you must also be a woman of the world, and familiar with such gatherings."

"You are right, sir, I am a musical performer, and nothing else. I play the piano and when I leave the stage, I cease to exist."

"Why, this is wonderful," he said softly. "A woman of mystery. What a challenge you will be!"

"Perhaps you had better be wary of me."

"Perhaps I had. And yet, of all lures, the hint of danger is the one most certain to entice a man on."

"And you think that's what I am trying to do? Entice you on?"

"I simply don't know. Are you the most honest woman I have ever known? Or the most coolly calculating?"

"You will have to decide that for yourself."

"Can't you stop playing that piano for one moment?"

"I am practising to be at my very best for tonight. How shocking if I were to play badly before the Duke?"

"I vouch for it, he will forgive you. For the moment I want your attention on me."

She laughed.

"You have as much of my attention as is necessary."

"Now that is sheer provocation. It's as good as telling me that I am dull."

"And you think you are a fascinating wit?"

"No lady has complained before."

"Ah, but I expect you have a great deal of money," she parried.

As she said this Carina looked up directly into his face and laughed aloud. He drew in his breath. Then he laughed with her.

"By heavens, I have never known a woman as daring as you," he said. "You are a challenge I must accept."

Carina brought her fingers down decisively on the keyboard.

"I am afraid I have no time for a challenge today," she replied coolly. "I have work to do, and it will occupy all my attention tonight."

"But eventually the performance will be over," he pointed out.

"Then I shall go to bed."

"Excellent!"

"To sleep," she said firmly, wondering if she was out of her mind to have embarked on this highly improper conversation.

"And now, I wish to leave. Will you move aside, please?"

He was leaning on the piano in such a way that there was very little room to get past him. For a moment she was afraid that he would block her path.

He smiled into her eyes in a way that was full of meaning.

He was dangerous, she thought. Not when he talked like a hardened seducer, but when he smiled with such tantalising warmth and promise. That was when a woman might weaken.

Always assuming that she was going to weaken.

Which she wasn't, she assured herself hastily.

Then he gave a sudden chuckle and, leaning over, kissed her on the mouth before she knew what he meant to do.

"The first round to me, I think," he said.

And he was gone before she could protest.

Carina's hands flew to her mouth in shock.

Then she fled to her room.

It was only for a moment that his lips had touched hers, but it had shaken her to the soul. A frisson of delight had gone through her, delight that she was sure no true lady could possibly feel.

She had been filled with the sweetness of pleasure and she knew that if he had kissed her for longer, she would have kissed him back. She would not have been able to help herself.

'I ought to be ashamed,' she murmured to herself 'ashamed.'

But she was not ashamed and she did not think she could force herself to be. For what else were men and women created, but to bring each other such happiness?

To calm herself Carina began to look through her clothes, trying to decide what to wear tonight.

At last she chose a very elegant pink dress. It was a ball gown, made of silk covered with tulle and decorated with flowers, each one touched with diamante so that it glittered when she moved.

She had bought it in a moment of extravagance, wondering if she could ever wear it.

Now she knew that she absolutely must wear it tonight with her mother's diamond necklace.

It was a little disconcerting to discover, when she put on the dress, that it was rather lower in the bosom than she remembered.

The thought of Lord Thornhill seeing her dressed like this and giving his seductive smile, made her blush.

She wondered if she should change into something

more modest, but Julia came rushing in and exclaimed at the sight of her.

"Oh yes, you look just like one of us. And that necklace makes it perfect."

Before they came downstairs Carina hastily slipped on her mask again.

"Oh, I forgot to tell you," Julia said. "We are invited to dinner after all, so you won't need your mask until later."

"I think I would prefer to wear it," Carina replied. "All this is very new to me."

Bertie met them at the foot of the stairs, full of excitement.

"I have told His Grace that tonight 'Iris' is the first lady of our troupe," he said. "And he wishes you to sit beside him at dinner."

Carina nearly gasped with horror. Obviously Lord Thornhill had told the Duke how she had spoken about him, and that had intrigued this villainous man into seeking her company.

"Bertie, I can't – "

"My dear, you cannot say no to the Duke. He is a very imperious man who insists on his own way at all times."

He saw Carina looking stubborn and said frantically.

"I do not want to offend so good a patron. You need only sit by him. *Please!*"

"All right," she said hastily. "Just this once."

The sun broke over Bertie's face. It was his nature to look no further than the next difficulty. This one had been overcome and that was all he asked.

But then he thought of something else.

"Perhaps if you could remove your mask – ?"

"Absolutely not," Carina retorted in a voice that

brooked no argument.

Bertie retired, defeated.

"Ready?" he asked, offering her his arm.

Carina took it, raised her head, and advanced with him into the drawing room.

At first she had only a confused impression of many men, standing around, drinking and laughing, their heads turning to look at the new arrivals.

Looking at *her,* she soon realised.

She tried to look around discreetly, hoping to see Lord Thornhill. For if the Duke became troublesome, surely he would intervene to protect her.

Doubtless he had repeated her remarks in all innocence, forgetting that his friend was a satyr who would ignore the ties of friendship in pursuit of fresh prey.

Lord Thornhill would protect her from the Duke. Surely she could trust to that.

"That's the Duke by the fireplace," Bertie murmured. "Here we go."

Carina walked the last few steps in a dream, her eyes fixed on the man Bertie had said was the Duke.

But he could not be the Duke.

He was Lord Thornhill.

Yet a man might have more than one title, and it had never occurred to her –

"Your Grace," Bertie said, "allow me to introduce Lady Iris, the newest and brightest member of our troupe."

He turned and gave her that same disturbing smile that she had seen that afternoon.

The next moment he had carried her hand to his lips.

"Madam," he said softly, "I cannot tell you what this meeting means to me."

CHAPTER FOUR

With an effort Carina regained her composure and forced herself to confront the Duke steadily.

"But there is no need for Your Grace to tell me," she said stoutly. "I can read every thought that is passing through your head at this moment."

"That's very clever of you," he said, still holding her hand. "Perhaps you are a magician?"

"Not at all, but I feel sure you can understand my thoughts too."

He nodded and his eyes gleamed.

"I fear your thoughts condemn me, madam."

"If they do, would that be an injustice?"

To her surprise he coloured slightly.

"Perhaps I deserve your censure," he said, lowering his voice. "Be assured I shall endeavour to make amends tonight."

He kissed her hand again, but as soon as he had done so, Carina removed it quickly with a graceful gesture. Her heart was beating madly and she hoped nobody had noticed her discomposure.

But more than anything she hoped that the Duke had not noticed.

She still needed time to come to terms with the incredible discovery she had made.

The boy who had called her 'beloved', and who had lived in her heart and mind all these years, was the same person as the Duke of Westbury, a rakish, hardened libertine.

She was trying to decide what to say when two other men came up and joined them.

"Come on, David," one of them said. "You can't keep *Bertie's Beauties* all to yourself. We want to meet this lovely lady and know what flower she represents."

"This is Lady Iris," Bertie said. "She is our pianist and I can assure you that the music she plays is as beautiful as she is herself."

"Lady Iris," Lord Bruno said loudly, bowing before Carina, "allow me to assure you that we are all your slaves."

"But you must not be," Carina exclaimed. "It is unfair to my sisters, who are all far more beautiful than I."

As she said 'my sisters', she indicated in the direction of the other girls. As she had hoped Lord Bruno was diverted.

"Let me give you a glass of champagne," the Duke offered.

Carina took the glass, but she had no intention of drinking it. She wanted to keep a clear head for her performance.

After Lord Bruno the men came crowding round, attracted by the mystery of her mask.

The Duke introduced her to Viscount Manton, who was far more gentlemanly than Lord Bruno. He bowed low but did not attempt to take her hand.

Now Carina had a chance to look around and realise that, apart from the young ladies of *Bertie's Beauties*, there were only men at this gathering.

Lord Bruno had done the round of the other girls without managing to find one who took to him. Now he returned to Carina.

"Lady Iris," he bawled, "why do you conceal yourself behind a mask?"

"That is the lady's business," the Duke said in a voice that would have been a warning to a more sensitive man.

"But how are we to know if she's really a beauty?" Bruno demanded. "I insist on knowing."

He reached out a hand towards Carina's face, but before he could touch her the Duke seized his wrist.

"Not so fast," he said. "A lady is entitled to keep her secrets. Drop your hand. *Drop it I say.*"

Lord Bruno was about to bluster it out, but he caught a look at the Duke's eyes and gasped. They were fierce and blazing, yet freezing cold at the same time. Before the unexpected menace in those eyes Bruno fell back, his hand drooping.

There was a nervous silence all around. Carina had not seen the Duke's expression, only its startling effect on Lord Bruno. The others, who had seen everything, exchanged glances. Everyone knew, of course, that the Duke was possessive, but nobody had seen anything like this before.

A lofty butler came to stand just inside the door.

"Dinner is served," he announced.

Immediately the Duke offered his arm to Carina, and together they walked into the dining room.

She almost gasped at the magnificence. There was a long, rosewood dining table, capable of seating twenty-four guests. Fine china and crystal was laid out and beautiful flower arrangements stretched down the centre.

Around the walls stood more footmen than she could count, all with powdered wigs and wearing the green and white livery of the Duke of Westbury.

The walls of the dining room were covered with

portraits, which Carina guessed must be of the family, as several of them bore a marked resemblance to the Duke.

He took his seat at the head of the table and placed Carina on his right.

On her other side was an elderly Marquis who introduced himself eagerly. They exchanged pleasantries about horses, until the Duke interrupted by saying,

"Lady Iris – I am being neglected. Chadwick, you old dog, find another lady to flirt with."

The elderly Marquis laughed and turned his attention to Julia, who was seated on his other side.

"How long have you been with Bertie?" the Duke asked Carina. "You were not performing last month when I visited him and arranged for him and his troupe to come here today."

"No, I am a new addition," Carina replied.

"How can he be so clever as to find beautiful women who never seem to come my way?"

Carina laughed.

"I am sure that is not true," she said. "A Duke must be a target for all women."

He made a wry grimace.

"Meaning that they pursue my title and not me. Truly, madam, I will never grow conceited in your company.

"But you are right, of course. I often wonder how many of those beautiful women would visit me if I was living in a cottage and had only one horse to ride, or perhaps it should be a donkey!"

Carina laughed and said,

"I suppose every wealthy man wonders whether a lady cares for him or his possessions. But if there is true feeling between them, surely his heart will tell him the answer."

"I had never thought of it like that," he admitted.

"I suppose women suffer the same," Carina said. "If a woman is thought very beautiful, living in the limelight, and even more beautiful if she is one of *Bertie's Beauties*, she will receive far more attention than a plain 'Miss' listening to a barrel-organ."

The Duke laughed.

"I can hardly imagine you doing that," he said.

"But of course I can," Carina retorted. "Just as you can imagine you yourself being just a Mister No-One and wondering if you would receive the same admiration as a Duke."

The Duke stared at her.

"You are very astute, madam. I never thought to hear anything like this from a – " he checked himself.

"From a show girl?" Carina asked lightly.

"You are quite unlike any show girl I have ever met," he said solemnly. "You say things that go deep. In fact, you are making me think in a way I have always avoided in the past."

"Of course you have, because it is frightening," Carina told him. "But at heart you know that you want to be loved for yourself and yourself alone, and for that you have to find someone who is not as thrilled as we are by your lovely castle.

"In fact, what you really need," she added as though considering the matter very seriously, "is the daughter of another Duke. If her father was very grand he might even look down on you, and then you would know that you were loved for yourself alone."

"Have you met any of the ducal daughters that are on the marriage market?" he enquired dryly.

"No."

"I thought not. I *have* met them, *all* of them. Heaven

help me! And let me recommend that you keep that piece of advice to yourself."

Carina chuckled at his aghast air.

"Well, I didn't know what they were like," she defended herself.

"Let me further tell you that if you think a Duke's daughter is any less ambitious than her untitled friends, you do not know the world. If anything, they are worse. If Papa is a Duke, how could they endure the mortification of settling for a mere Marquis? It would be social catastrophe."

"I hadn't thought of that," she admitted. "My commiserations, Your Grace. I had not realised that you led such a hard life."

He smiled his appreciation

"Little witch!" he said. "I am tempted to follow Bruno's example and remove that tantalising mask."

Carina faced him steadily.

"Lord Bruno behaved as he did because he is an ungentlemanly boor," she said. "I wonder what your reason could be."

"You are very daring, Lady Iris."

She smiled.

"I don't think so. You see, I do trust you to behave like a gentleman."

"That's a very unfair thing to say. Now I have to behave myself whether I want to or not."

"Are you saying that I couldn't have trusted you otherwise?" she asked.

He was silent with an odd, arrested look in his eyes.

"Do you know," he said at last, "I am not sure that I could ever trust myself to behave well with you."

"But I have no doubts about it," she said. "I feel perfectly safe."

This was far from being true. There was something about the Duke that was dangerous to all women. Carina felt it and responded to it with a kind of shocked excitement. But instinct told her that to put this man on his honour was the best way to defend herself.

"You must have had many men at your feet," he observed, "since you are so skilled in duelling with them."

"Duelling with a man doesn't bring him to a woman's feet," Carina replied. "On the contrary. Men like silly women so that they can feel superior."

"Do you speak from experience, madam?"

She gave him a fervent look through the slits in her mask, which were, however, large enough for him to see the deep blue of her eyes.

"I can be *incredibly* silly when I decide to be," she assured him.

"And so you use your skills to overcome all men?"

She smiled and did not answer, concentrating on her plate, which was filled with delicious food.

"Tell me," the Duke insisted.

"No," she said calmly. "A lady should never be so indelicate as to discuss one man with another."

"But we are not talking about one man, but many," he replied. "They send you roses and jewels, don't they? Wherever you go, they pursue you?"

She looked him straight in the eye.

"I will not discuss this with you, Your Grace," she said in a voice that was little more than a whisper, but which astonished him with its iron determination.

At last the Duke said,

"But we will discuss it – at some other time."

"Perhaps."

"Not perhaps. We will. I want to know everything about you, every thought and feeling you have ever had. I want to know where you've lived, what you've done and your plans for the future."

"My plans for the future are very simple," Carina said. "I intend to perform for you to the best of my ability and then to vanish."

He looked at her intently.

"I won't let you vanish."

She laughed.

"I shall not ask you," she said sweetly. "I shall simply do as I please. I always do."

"And suppose I demand that you do what pleases me?"

"Oh no! I never yield to demands."

"And I never beg," he said at once, "whether of a woman or a man. I take what I want and in the end I always get my way. But I don't mind playing your game in the meantime."

Carina smiled at him.

"We shall see," she said. "Tonight I know you and your guests want to laugh and be entertained, and nothing else, for the moment, is of any importance."

Having said that, she turned deliberately to talk to the Marquis on her other side, leaving the Duke no choice but to follow her example.

She was astonished at herself for addressing him in such a way. But of course, she suddenly realised, it was not Carina who had spoken so, but Lady Iris.

Iris was a brilliant, unconventional creature with men at her feet all over the country, eager to offer her roses and jewels – the Duke himself had said so. And in her superb self-confidence she regarded the Duke as just another admirer and did not scruple to let him see as much.

It was heady, thrilling wine and she felt she could get used to it with dangerous ease.

Towards the end of the meal, following a signal from Bertie, the performers rose while the other guests were still drinking their coffee.

"You must excuse me, Your Grace," Carina said to the Duke. "We must prepare for the performance."

She would have risen but he detained her, seizing her hand and dropping a kiss on the back.

"Ah yes, the performance," he said. "I am looking forward to – many things."

"Your Grace," she whispered urgently. "You must let me go."

"For now I will. But remember that I always get my way," he added with soft emphasis, looking into her eyes with a kind of fierce intensity, as though he would hypnotise her into agreeing with him.

But Carina had too much strength of mind to fall under such a deliberate spell. She regarded him with her head on one side.

"Even if the lady is not willing, Your Grace?"

"But the lady is always willing, I assure you."

He kissed her hand again, letting his lips linger caressingly, so that flurries of pleasure soared through her.

But at the same time Carina was becoming angry. How dare he use his position of power to overcome her! The fact that his touch delighted her only made his behaviour more disgraceful.

In her fury she dared to say,

"Ah yes, I was forgetting your coronet and your vast wealth."

His eyes flashed a warning. Carina pulled her hand free, rose from her seat and fled.

As she hurried to the music room, she was intensely conscious of the place on her hand where he had kissed her and which seemed to be tingling.

But she was even more conscious of the warmth that suffused her at their whole encounter. Seductive as his touch was, their verbal sparring had thrilled her even more. She had challenged him and at least she had not come off the worst.

He had actually admitted that she had made him think, and she guessed that was something that did not happen very often. A man so rich and privileged did not need to think.

In the music room chairs had been arranged in a semi-circle around that part of the floor where the artistes would sing and dance. The piano stood on a raised dais just behind them.

The costumes had been moved into two small rooms at the rear of the stage, and several servants had been deputed to help them with the quick changes.

The girls were to start the performance in blue satin dresses, with a multitude of sequins that flashed as they moved. The boys were in evening dress, all looking very handsome.

They did a few turns about the floor, judging their space. Bertie pronounced himself satisfied, and they vanished into the next room, ready to make their entrance.

"Now all we need is our audience," Bertie announced in a voice that revealed how much he loved his theatre. "And here they come."

Two powdered footmen pulled open the double doors and the gentlemen began to stream in.

"Are you ready?" Bertie whispered in Carina's ear.

"Oh my goodness!" she said suddenly. "I can't do this."

"Nonsense, my dear of course you can," he said gently. "You are going to be wonderful."

He squeezed her hand and she looked into his eyes, finding such kindness that her fears fled.

Taking a deep breath she walked onto the dais, turned to face the audience and curtsied low.

There was the Duke, in the centre of the semi-circle, his eyes fixed on her with intense interest.

Carina seated herself at the piano and struck up the introduction.

At once the troupe came whirling out onto the floor, the girls flaunting their pretty sparkling dresses and giving knowing looks over their shoulders at the men in the audience.

Then the girls began to sing.

"Please to welcome Bertie's Beauties,
We are flowers, everyone one.
We dance and twirl with every breeze,
And we're ever so much fun."

The boys echoed,

"And they're ever so much fun."

The girls took up the melody again.

"We emerge with every morning,
We're the flowers of the dawning.
If you sprinkle us with dew,
We can be good fun for you."

Again the boys echoed the last line, slipping their arms around the girls' waists and giving them knowing looks, which were duly returned.

Carina had never heard the words before and was thankful that her aunt was not here to listen. She would certainly never have approved.

The troupe were skilled performers but there was a

slightly improper note or action in everything they said and everything they did.

The song continued,

"We are flowers of the noonday,
When the sun is at its height.
But if you are true and we like you too,
We are flowers of the night."

After a few more turns they all waltzed off, leaving Carina hoping that the mask was hiding her blushes.

The audience roared their approval of the double meanings and clapped loudly.

Carina remembered Bertie telling her, "you'll find the applause irresistible, as we all do."

He was right, she thought. It was a thrilling experience, sweeping her up on a tide of excitement that she felt might carry her anywhere.

Pansy came on alone and sang a clever ditty. Without being blatant, it was very saucy and she gave every word its full emphasis, which was much appreciated by every man in the audience.

By now the other two girls had changed their costumes into something a little more daring. They performed a dance, to the delight of the audience. The boys in the troupe came on to dance with them.

With three boys and two girls there was a lot of by-play as the girls tried to decide between them. Finally one man was left alone on stage. He shrugged in comic despair and went off alone.

Judging by the applause and the roars of laughter from the audience, Bertie had certainly provided them with something they would not forget in a hurry.

As the performance ended and the troupe were bowing and curtsying, Bertie appeared to take his own applause, making extravagant gestures, obviously in seventh heaven.

Carina watched his enjoyment, smiling. There was something innocent, almost childlike, about Bertie's pleasure and like the others in the troupe, she too had become fond of him.

Then to her surprise Bertie walked towards the piano, took her hand, and led her forward to present her to the audience, who shouted their appreciation.

As they clapped she curtsied to them, exhilarated. Her fellow artistes were also applauding, showing their gratitude to her for saving them. The men in the audience crowded round her at the foot of the dais, cheering her to the echo.

Only one man did not join the throng and that was the Duke. He stayed back, his eyes fixed on her, telling her silently that he was not one of the common herd, but that she was his, nonetheless.

And Lady Iris looked back at him from behind her mask, her eyes gleaming, telling him silently not to be so sure of himself.

Then footmen appeared bearing drinks for audience and performers alike and suddenly there was a party.

In moments every girl was surrounded by the men, including Carina.

"Excuse me," Bertie said, elbowing his way through and drawing her aside.

"I promised that you would not be exposed to this," he murmured. "So would you like to slip away now? Otherwise you might be a little embarrassed by what you hear."

"Is it very naughty?" Carina teased.

"It can get very naughty indeed," Bertie said carefully. "Not at all the kind of thing you are used to, so perhaps you'd better be off going to bed."

"How kind of you," Carina said. "I think – ".

The Duke was watching her, his eyes dark and brilliant.

"I think – perhaps I should stay for a short while," she said. "I am sure they'll behave themselves like gentlemen."

"I wish I was that sure," Bertie growled. "You really should go, my dear, before it gets – a little – a little – " he appeared about to expire with embarrassment.

"A little – ?"

"A little naughty," he said desperately.

"I'll stay for just a while," Carina murmured, hardly aware of Bertie any more.

The Duke was moving slowly towards her, taking her hand.

"Goodbye, Bertie," he said firmly.

Bertie retreated, reluctantly.

"Congratulations, madam," the Duke said politely. "You have been the success of the evening. Your playing was brilliant."

"You are too kind, sir," Carina replied. "But we both know that brilliant is far too strong a word. The pianist's job is to fade into the background."

"Which you could never do. You are a beauty among beauties, as well you know."

"I know no such thing."

"Then it will be my pleasure to explain it to you at great length."

"Please don't," she said at once. "If there is one subject that bores me more than any other, it is myself."

"Then you are an extraordinary woman, Lady Iris. Most women can talk of nothing else but themselves."

She laughed.

"But a really clever man always knows how to turn the conversation around to *him*self."

"Then I cannot be a clever man, because, like you, I find myself an intolerable bore."

"Dear me!" she exclaimed. "Whatever will we talk about? Perhaps we should each go in search of the others."

His eyes gleamed.

"Very clever," he murmured. "But I will not allow you to leave my side."

"And I will not allow you to give me orders. Don't forget that I am here as part of a troupe, hired to entertain everyone."

"Hired by me," he reminded her.

"You mean that he who pays the piper, calls the tune? Then I must tell Your Grace that I am not really a member of this troupe. I am a last minute replacement for a girl who was injured and I shall not be accepting any money for this engagement.

"So, my Lord Duke, you do not pay this piper, and therefore will not call my tune. Now, will you excuse me?"

She gave him the smallest possible curtsy and turned away. Her attention was immediately claimed by three other men, who all clamoured for her to remove her mask.

They accepted her refusal gracefully enough and she realised that there was safety in numbers. One man was dangerous. Three would watch each other to ensure that no one man gained an advantage.

And the Duke himself protected her, keeping a watchful eye on them all and making sure that they knew he was there. Gradually the other men understood that Lady Iris belonged to His Grace and their demeanour became more respectful.

Carina thought that if she had really been interested in

one of them, she might have been annoyed by the way the Duke put a blight on their admiration.

As it was, she had to admit to herself that he eclipsed every man there.

She was annoyed at his self-assurance, but that did not prevent her from being fascinated by him. There was a thrill in knowing that the other girls sought in vain to catch his eye, but he was interested only in her.

She had wanted excitement, and now she was getting more than she had ever dreamed possible.

She felt like Cinderella at the ball. When the clock struck twelve it would all be over. The beautiful dresses would vanish, the spell would end.

But until then she was going to enjoy every moment.

A servant appeared and went to the piano. He had been summoned to play for anyone who wanted to dance.

But he played very badly and after a moment Carina touched him on the shoulder and took over.

Then the dancing really got under way as she played waltzes and polkas tirelessly for an hour. Glancing up she saw chagrin on the Duke's face at the way she had thwarted him yet again.

She guessed that he was planning to waylay her later.

But she had no intention of playing the game his way. She had one final trick up her sleeve.

Waiting until somebody had claimed the Duke's attention, she left the piano, blew Bertie a kiss and then took his advice by slipping away to bed.

She lay awake for a long time, trying to think about the incredible things that had happened to her tonight. But she found she could not think. She could only feel. And all her feelings were concentrated on the Duke.

Happiness, sadness, anger, regret, all these were mixed

up together. The sadness would come soon enough, she knew. She must go away and never see him again. But before then, she would squeeze every last moment of joy out of this wonderful occasion and then live on it for the rest of her life.

At last she dozed off, but then woke again suddenly. There was a new quality in the silence of the night, something strange that made her get out of bed and go to the French windows.

Pulling them open, she stepped out onto the small balcony outside. There she raised her eyes to the brilliant moon, and drank in the beauty of the night.

Gradually she became aware that she was no longer alone. Looking down, she saw a man sitting on a low stone wall, gazing up at her.

It was the Duke.

Carina gasped and raised her hands to her face, fearful that he would recognise her as the girl he had met in the theatre long ago.

But then she realised that she was just as hidden now as she had been behind her mask.

The distance concealed her, so did the night, and her hair hanging about her face.

"I came to tell you that I'm sorry," he said. "I spoke to you in an ungentlemanly way, and I ask your pardon."

Carina smiled.

"Are you smiling?" he asked. "I can't see properly.

"Yes, I am smiling."

"Then you are no longer angry with me? I am forgiven?"

"Yes, you are forgiven."

"And you will still be here tomorrow?"

Carina hesitated while a warning cried aloud in her head.

'*Go away from here. If you stay, your heart will be broken.*'

But would it not be worth the heartbreak, for a few hours of joy to last her all her life?

"Tell me," the Duke insisted from below. "Say that you will stay."

She looked down.

"I will stay," she promised. "For a while."

"And then?"

"And then – when it's time for me to leave, I shall leave. Goodnight Your Grace."

She withdrew into her room and closed the glass doors firmly.

But she could not be as strong as she meant to be. After pacing the floor for a few moments, she hurried back out onto the balcony.

But the spot where he had stood was empty. It was as though he had never been there and maybe her fevered mind had imagined everything.

She stood watching and listening.

But all about her there was nothing but the moonlight and the wind whispering through the trees.

CHAPTER FIVE

The next morning the performers were served breakfast on their own in a room next to the dining room, while the Duke and his friends had theirs in the dining room itself.

Carina, when she came down for breakfast, heard them laughing. She was sure she could single out the Duke's laughter from the others and hurried past lest she be tempted to linger.

With everything in her she longed to see him, but she knew it would be considered improper for a show girl to seek him out and he must not see her without the mask.

Over breakfast she listened to the chatter of the other performers and learnt that the girls and Bertie himself had enjoyed whatever had happened to keep them up so late.

She guessed from the way one or two of them spoke that some of the things which had been said and done were best not remembered, or at least, best not spoken about.

After they had eaten breakfast, Carina moved into the sitting room they had been allotted. It was a comfortable room full of bookshelves with French windows leading onto the garden. Some of the performers were there, lolling, half-asleep on sofas and chairs.

"Are you going to see the racing?" she asked Julia.

"No, let the men do that," Julia replied. "I am too tired to walk and I'm going to sleep if I get the chance, before we put on our show this evening."

She fanned herself languidly, already apparently on the verge of nodding off.

Bertie came in, also barely suppressing his yawns.

"What a night!" he exclaimed. "What a night!"

"Do you mean the performance or afterwards?" Julia asked wickedly.

"Please, madam!" Bertie said, feigning shock. "We'll have none of that sort of talk."

"We just couldn't help noticing that there are some very pretty housemaids," Samson observed slyly.

"Yes, I noticed *you* noticing a very pretty housemaid," Bertie retorted. "And I was shocked! *Shocked!*"

Everyone shouted with laughter. Carina wondered at herself for not blushing over such a frank conversation. But everyone seemed so friendly and pleasant that it did not seem anything out of the ordinary.

Suddenly, from the next room, came the Duke's voice.

"Bertie! Are you there?"

"I'm in here," Bertie called.

Dismayed, Carina realised that the Duke was about to enter and see her without her mask. The situation was desperate, and she reacted as quick as a flash.

"Excuse me," she muttered to Julia, whisking her fan out of her hand so fast that Julia was left waving at empty air.

Carina moved backwards to the French windows that looked out onto the garden and went to stand half in, half out. In this way she could see the Duke and hear what was said, while concealing most of her face.

Also the balcony gave onto a flight of steps that led down into the garden and which she could use to escape if necessary.

The next moment he was in the room, a worried frown on his face. Carina stood back, half hidden by the curtains, keeping the fan up and trying not to let her heart beat so wildly.

"What has happened, Your Grace?" Bertie asked. "You are looking worried."

"I am worried," the Duke answered, "and I need your help."

"We'll do all we can to help you," Bertie promised. "But after last night's success, I cannot believe that anything terrible has happened."

"It is not exactly terrible but very difficult," the Duke replied. "Yesterday, at almost the last moment, I was asked if I would have a Ladies' Race, where in the past I have only had gentlemen. Because I did not want to offend Lady Palmer, who is very important in this part of the country, I agreed they should have a race today.

"I understand that there are as many as eighteen entries, which I did not expect, and after running in the race they expect to come to dinner tonight. What's more, they have heard of your show, and want to see it."

There was a silence.

"Oh dear!" Bertie said at last.

"Exactly!" the Duke replied. "That was my own reaction, although I expressed it more strongly. Although they will enjoy your performance, they will be shocked by some of it, and I've no intention, after waiting so long to have you here, to have your performance spoilt by Lady Palmer or anyone else."

Carina spoke up from behind the fan.

"Will Lady Palmer be accompanied by many respectable ladies?"

"A whole rabbit warren of them," the Duke groaned

and everyone laughed at the expression.

"Then there's only one way out," Carina said. "We shall have to make the show more sedate."

"How can we possibly do that?" Bertie demanded.

"By changing the words of some of the songs," she replied.

The Duke was watching her, as if trying to decide if this mystery woman was the same one who had entranced him last night. At last a slow smile came over his face and she thought he gave a faint nod in her direction.

"Can you do it in the time?" he asked.

"I can," she said with a confidence that came from she knew not where. "And Bertie will re-work the dances so that they are less – you know."

"I do know," he agreed, his lips twitching. "Can you do that, Bertie?"

"Of course I can," he asserted at once. "Lady Iris, you are brilliant. Come on, all of you."

"I was going to enjoy a good sleep today," Julia complained.

Laughing, Bertie helped her to her feet. Then he held out his other hand to Carina.

"Let me escort you, Lady Iris," he said.

But a cough from behind him drew his attention.

"Goodbye, Bertie," the Duke said.

"Oh, yes Your Grace, I was just – "

"Goodbye, Bertie."

Bertie and Julia slid diplomatically away.

The Duke leaned one arm on the door frame, looking at Carina speculatively. She kept the fan firmly in place.

"Today you show me your eyes," he said. "Yesterday I saw only your mouth."

"So now you have seen my whole face," she replied, "and so you know what I look like."

"That isn't true. I know two disconnected halves, but only the whole face will tell me the complete story."

"You mean you've forgotten my mouth," she teased.

"Oh no, I could never forget your mouth. I remember clearly that it's the most beautiful, kissable mouth that any woman ever had. I told you that once before. Now I mean it ten times as much."

"I do not think you should discuss my mouth like that," she said demurely.

"No, what I ought to do is kiss it", replied the Duke. "And I will if you'll let me."

"But I won't," she said at once.

"Then you do me wrong, madam. A mouth like yours should be kissed and kissed often, by a man who is an expert in the art of kissing."

"Perhaps one day I shall meet such a man – "

"You have met him already and you know it. Why do you try to deny the truth?"

"I – " Carina tried to reply but the words would not come.

She gave thanks for the fan which hid most of her face. Otherwise he would surely be able to see how delightfully exciting she found this conversation.

Her conscience told her that everything they were saying was most improper and she should be ashamed for even joining in, much less enjoying it.

But she could not help herself. To be standing here with this thrillingly attractive man, discussing the prospect of his kissing her, was the most wonderful thing that had ever happened in her dull life. It sent tremors of warmth scurrying through her, making her feel light-headed.

"You know that it is your destiny to be kissed," he sighed, "and mine to kiss you."

"I know no such thing. I have my own plans – "

"If you are thinking of another man, forget him. I won't allow it."

"*You* won't – ?"

"You belong to me, don't you know that? I, and I alone, will kiss you," he insisted.

"Indeed, sir? And suppose I do not permit you to kiss me? Suppose I have another destiny in mind?"

"A woman's destiny is with a man, especially a woman like you. You were made for the art of love."

"I am an artiste," Carina teased, looking at him over the fan. "I live for music, and nothing else."

"That is not true," he murmured.

"Do you call a lady a liar? Fie, sir!"

"This lady has been deceiving me since the moment we met. She rejoices in it."

Carina laughed softly, and allowed her eyes to tease him over the rim of the fan.

"Very well," he said, "if you wish to play with me, I will allow it, for a while. But the time will come – "

"The time will never come," she interrupted him firmly.

But she was not sure whom she was trying to convince. Him – or herself.

"You think you can live only for your art?" he asked.

"I think that art is more important than love," she replied.

"I could change your mind," he breathed.

"No man will change my mind. I have a very strong mind. It never changes."

"Heaven preserve me from strong-minded women," he growled.

"I know, they're a great problem," she agreed. "They have this unfortunate tendency to say no, when you want them to say yes."

"I can bide my time. In the game we are playing there can be only one winner."

"Indeed. And the winner will be whichever of us is the more skilled and subtle."

"And you think that is yourself?"

"My Lord Duke, I know you to be many things, strong, powerful, splendid. But subtle? No."

"By heavens, madam, you are daring," he exclaimed.

"I am honest. Is that to be daring?"

"If I am as powerful as you say, it might be – a little dangerous."

"There's more than one kind of danger."

"Indeed there is," he murmured. "I thought of you all last night. I thought of how your body would feel in my arms, how your lips would feel against mine, soft, parting, yielding."

Carina tried to shut out the agreeable pictures this created. She would not let him win. She *must* not.

"Let me see your face," he commanded.

"Sir, I will not."

His eyes gleamed suddenly. Carina read his purpose in them and dodged away, running quickly down the little flight of steps that led down from the balcony to the garden.

She ran without looking behind her, but soon she was sure that he was not following her and slowed down. There was no sign of him.

She had escaped, but in her heart she knew that she did

not truly want to escape this fascinating man, whose words seemed to open a new and brilliant world.

But that world was not for her, she reminded herself. No decent girl could accept the terms he was offering.

Then she pulled herself together and told herself sternly that she must forget him. She was now an artiste and she had work to do.

Before joining Bertie and the others she ran up to her room and collected her mask, just in case the Duke should surprise them again. Then she walked downstairs and found the troupe in the music room.

As soon as she entered Carina became aware of a curious 'something' in the air. Everyone turned and looked at her with great interest.

"We were not expecting to see you for a long time," Helen said.

There was a faint edge to her voice that Carina had not heard before. Some of the others concealed smiles.

Bertie moved quickly to avert an incident.

"Thank goodness you're here. Now we can get to work. I hope you have plenty of ideas for changing the songs."

"First let me return Julia's fan," Carina said. "Thank you Julia. I am sorry to have whisked it away from you like that."

"Not at all," Julia replied. "His Grace doesn't appeal to me anyway."

"I – don't know what you mean."

"Don't be shy," Samson said. "We all think you are being very clever, the way you use that mask. Extremely subtle. Just the way to lure a man on."

"But I – "

"Can we start work?" Bertie cried quickly. "Lady Iris,

what about the first song?"

Seizing Carina's hand he drew her to the piano, murmuring,

"Ignore Helen. She's jealous. She wanted the Duke for herself."

"Bertie – "

"And I think you're very clever to keep wearing that mask, just in case he comes in. In fact, I have brought some more for you, from the company stock."

He opened a box which contained five other masks and Carina quickly selected a plain one, made of black satin.

"Thank you, Bertie," she whispered. "That was very thoughtful."

He held her hand between his for a moment.

"He is a very handsome man, Lady Iris," he whispered so that the others could not hear. "But – "

"Don't worry. I am in no danger of losing my head or my heart. I'm just playing the game like a good *Bertie's Beauty*."

"I'm so glad to hear it, except that a well brought up young lady like yourself is not supposed to know how the game is played."

Carina gave a soft chuckle. "But you would be surprised how many new games I've learned since I've been with you."

Bertie smiled and backed away. As he moved, he muttered to himself,

"I don't think I would be surprised. Oh, Lady Iris, please be careful."

For an hour they all worked hard, making the show more sedate. Carina discovered that she had a real gift for words and managed to tone down the songs so that everyone was satisfied. But there was one song that defeated even her.

"You can't take out the *double entendres*," she told Bertie, "because the whole song is built on them."

"Then we'll have to omit the song altogether," he replied.

"Won't that leave the show a bit short?" Samson wanted to know.

"Yes, we need an extra item."

"If you want us to learn something new – " Julia began in a rebellious tone.

"Just one more little thing," he begged.

"Perhaps I can fill in with a piano solo," Carina suggested.

Everyone fell on this suggestion with relief.

"Are you sure it won't be too tiring for you?" Bertie asked her solicitously. "You will be playing all the time."

"I enjoy playing. Don't worry about me."

"But I do worry about you," said Bertie quietly. "You are so good and kind, and we take advantage of you."

"Nonsense," Carina laughed.

"It isn't nonsense," he said, suddenly serious. "I can't help feeling that I've harmed you. When I asked you to help out, I never imagined – that is – "

"I can take care of myself," she assured him.

"I hope so, but this isn't really the kind of entertainment a refined young lady should see, never mind take part in. If your aunt knew, she would have the vapours."

"Then we must make sure she doesn't find out. Her servants only know that I left with you, not what I was planning to do."

She paused for a moment before she added,

"By the way, please don't tell His Grace who I really am. If you do, he is certain to mention it to my aunt when they meet in the future. And when I have left here, I certainly do not intend to say anything."

"That's very sensible of you," Bertie replied. "Of course I promise. I would not hurt you for the world, Lady Iris. You do believe that, don't you?"

"Of course I do," she said, a little surprised by a touch of fervour in his voice that she did not understand.

At that moment the Duke appeared in the doorway. Helen simpered, but he did not notice her. His eyes were fixed on Carina, who hastily checked that her black satin mask was in place.

"My new guests will be arriving at any moment," he said. "Before they do, I want to thank you for your splendid efforts. I have arranged for lunch to be served to you here."

"If Your Grace will permit me," Carina said, "I would like to go up on to the roof to watch the races when they take place."

"Of course," the Duke agreed. "Take my binoculars with you. They are the very finest that can be bought, and they'll give you a good view. You will find them in the hall."

"Thank you so much," Carina said, smiling at him.

He smiled back as he said,

"My compliments, madam. You played absolutely brilliantly last night and I enjoyed every note."

He spoke with courteous formality, just as though he had not been whispering words of passion to her only an hour earlier.

Carina took her cue from him and replied,

"You are too kind, Your Grace. "I was so afraid that Bertie might find me too countrified."

"Now you are asking for compliments," the Duke retorted. "You know you played brilliantly, and it surprises me that you are not a professional."

"I am quite happy to play in the country when it is in such a beautiful place as this castle," she replied.

"You are most gracious to say so," the Duke said. "Thank you all for making last night a great success and I am relying on you to do the same this evening."

"We will try," Carina promised, "and we will have to hope that the ladies are not too disappointed."

"Disappointed?" the Duke echoed, startled. "Why should they be? Surely you have made the show respectable?"

"Of course, but think what they must have heard about us already."

Bertie began to laugh.

"She's right. They are coming for the pleasure of being shocked. Which means they will be disappointed when we don't shock them."

The Duke was laughing too.

"Well, there's nothing we can do about it," he said. "They'll just have to go away thinking what a virtuous man I am. It will make a refreshing change."

"Personally," Bertie said, raising his eyes to heaven, "I think the virtuous country folk should keep to the country. And the ones who enjoy what I give them should keep their mouths shut."

They all laughed heartily and the Duke left the room.

Bertie sighed.

"It must be hard work being a Duke if every time you want something amusing and private, the goody-goodies of the county burst in on you."

"Be honest Bertie," Samson said, "that doesn't happen to us very often."

More laughter and now the footmen were bringing in the lunch, which they all fell on hungrily. Carina had a quick snack, then left the room and went to the hall to collect the Duke's binoculars.

She climbed up the main staircase and then up the narrow stairway which led her on to the top of the castle.

The sun was bright and she thought it was very exciting to be at such a height and to have such a magnificent view in every direction.

Looking one way she could see in the distance the little village with the church prominent in the centre. Also the main road on which there were a number of shops.

Turning the other way she could see the vast acres of land owned by the Duke. There was a stream running through the middle where she was sure, if he ever had time, he would catch several fish.

Then she looked to the left, where she could see the flat field on which he had built the small, private race course. Already people were arriving. She could see the Duke riding towards the course, mounted on a magnificent black steed. Beside him was a very pretty young woman. At least, Carina thought she was pretty. It was hard to make out details at this distance.

She raised the binoculars to her eyes and found that they really were as excellent as the Duke had said. Everything was crystal sharp and much enlarged.

Then she dropped them again, wishing that she had not seen so much.

The young lady was indeed very pretty. She was more than pretty, she was entrancingly beautiful. And she was talking and laughing with the Duke in a very animated and familiar way.

Suddenly the sun seemed to go in, and the day was less bright.

Carina did not want to look, but somehow she couldn't stop herself raising the glasses and watching the girl again.

She saw her burst into laughter at something the Duke had said and lean her head close to his.

There was a little flutter in Carina's heart.

A marquee had been set up, adorned with colourful flags. Inside, Carina guessed, food was being served as everyone was going in. As she watched, the Duke dismounted and held up his arms to assist his pretty companion to dismount.

When she was on the ground he offered her his arm, and the two of them walked into the marquee together.

Carina knew that she should go away and not see any more. But she could not force herself to leave. She kept the binoculars trained on the entrance in case the Duke emerged again.

At last he did and now she could see the pretty lady more clearly. She was hanging on the Duke's arm, laughing up into his face.

Carina closed her eyes.

Men on horseback were cantering to the starting line. Carina picked out Lord Bruno and the Duke, and several of the others that she recognised from last night.

There was the crack of a pistol and they were off. It was immediately clear that the Duke was the finest rider in the field. His magnificent black stallion shot ahead of the rest of the field. Carina watched with delight as he passed the winning post.

Everyone crowded around him, including the lovely lady, who presented him with a trophy. He kissed her hand and the crowd cheered.

Then it was the Ladies' Race, and the Duke's pretty companion lined up at the start. She was a fine rider, Carina noticed, but she was sure that she herself could have done better, as she knew that she rode superbly.

How she longed to be there, speeding ahead of the others, knowing that the Duke was admiring her.

If only she could have been that girl, crossing the finishing line, receiving the applause, being handed down from her horse by the Duke.

But she knew it could never be her.

This, she thought, was what it must be like to be the 'unofficial love' of such a man. It would mean existing only for his leisure moments. The rest of the time it would mean being forced to watch him with some other woman, one that he could introduce to the world, because he was not ashamed of her.

'No-one could possibly want such a life,' she told herself. 'However attractive he is. I am playing a game which will soon be over. As long as I remember that, no harm will be done. But I know if I am honest with myself that I cannot afford to let it go on too long.'

Then the sound of his voice came back to her, saying, *"You belong to me, don't you know that?"*

It was true. She did belong to him. But he could never belong to her.

As she descended from the roof, she was aware of a strange pain in her heart that had never been there before.

CHAPTER SIX

For the rest of the afternoon Carina was occupied working out a little song for the evening's performance. So she did not see the party return to the castle and was spared the sight of the Duke and his young lady.

But she did not escape entirely. Going quietly down to the music room, she stopped on the staircase just as the guests appeared in the hall below, ready to go into the dining room.

They were all in evening dress, the men in tails, the women in gorgeous silks and satins. Carina stepped back into the shadows, horribly conscious of her unfashionable dress.

The elderly housekeeper was coming down the stairs just behind her.

"Can I help you miss?" she asked kindly.

"Oh no, I was just looking – "

"They're beautiful, aren't they?" the old woman said with a sentimental sigh. "Especially Lady Virginia."

"Is she the one in the pink dress, holding the Duke's arm?" Carina asked her.

"That's right, miss. Lady Virginia Chesterham. Her father is the Earl of Chesterham. They live only a few miles from here. Such a lovely young lady. I am really looking forward to the day when she is the mistress here."

Something lurched in Carina's breast and she clung to

the balustrade for support.

"You mean – that she and the Duke are betrothed?" she managed to say.

"Oh no, nothing has been announced, but we're all sure that it's just a matter of time."

At that moment the Duke looked up. Carina started back against the wall, hoping that he hadn't seen her.

"I must go," she murmured.

"Yes, miss. They're going in to dinner now, and from now on the servants are going to be busier than ever."

Carina sped back upstairs. There was no chance now to practise her song. It was too risky.

Bertie met her in the corridor.

"It'll soon be time to get dressed for the performance," he said. "Why, Lady Iris, what is it? You are looking so pale. Are you ill?"

"No, don't worry Bertie. I'm not going to get sick and leave you in the lurch."

"I wasn't thinking of that," he said gently. "I was worried about you. You look as though you're about to faint."

"Well, I am not," she said, pulling herself together. "I've got a lovely new song for tonight, and I am going to give a performance that will make you proud of me."

"I have no doubt that I will be proud of you. I only wish you were coming further with us. I have just received a telegram."

He produced a piece of paper from his pocket and waved it at her.

"An engagement," he said. "Potentially, at any rate."

"That's wonderful. Another great house?"

"No, in London, at a little supper club that's just

opened. They've heard of us and want us to go straight there and show them what we can do. If they like it, it will mean leaving tonight and going to collect Melanie. I dare say you'll be glad to get back, eh?"

"Oh – yes," she replied, dismayed.

To leave tonight, so suddenly. She had counted on just a little longer.

But perhaps this was for the best.

"They're having dancing after the show," Bertie said. "With any luck we'll be invited to join, and I can circulate and drum up some more business for later in the year. But after that we'll have to be off."

"Yes," said Carina in a hollow voice.

"Now, about tonight's performance, will you be wearing the same dress as last night?"

"No," she said decidedly. "I am going to ask one of the other girls to lend me something really glorious."

"Good for you! But don't ask Helen. She's ready to murder you!"

It was Julia who showed her the perfect dress. Luckily they were the same size and the dazzling silver creation fitted Carina exactly.

She thought of Lady Virginia, in her pink satin dress and the pearl tiara on her head. An Earl's daughter, dressed up to entice a proposal from a Duke.

Some instinct told her that there was no betrothal. The families might have made their plans and the servants might be hoping, but the Duke had not uttered the vital words. She was sure of it.

From her mother's jewel box she took a diamond necklace and a matching diamond tiara, the most valuable jewellery that she possessed. When they were in place she chose a silver spangled mask and slipped it on.

84

Suddenly she felt like a warrior, spurred and helmeted for battle.

For it was a kind of battle. A battle to make him aware of her, once and for all, as a woman, before he returned to his life and she returned to hers.

A light supper was served to the performers.

"He never forgets us," Bertie said happily. "You should see the way some of the aristocracy behave. But His Grace is a true gentleman."

When the meal was finished they hurried down to the music room. Peering through a crack in the door they saw that the audience was already in place.

In the centre of the front row sat the Duke, with Lady Virginia beside him, giving him a sideways, flirtatious glance.

As the performers entered, Carina saw at once that the flowers had been added to since the previous evening.

Roses were piled up around the piano stool, so that she appeared to be sitting on a throne of flowers.

'He ordered this,' she thought. 'I just know he did.'

She thought as she sat down that her dress blended beautifully with the flowers, especially the roses. She knew that the lights were glittering on her tiara, and she thought perhaps she was shining as though she had just stepped down to earth from the sun. At any rate, she hoped the Duke thought so.

She struck up the introduction, the girls swirled onto the stage in their lovely dresses and began to sing. It was the same song as last night, but with certain crucial changes.

"Please to welcome Bertie's Beauties,
We are flowers, yes we are.
We dance and twirl with every breeze,
Whether near or whether far."

Every single risqué reference had been removed. What was left was an innocuous little song about nothing in particular.

The girls were moving differently too. There were no sideways glances at the audience, no winks and no suggestive smiles. It would not have offended a nun.

At the end of the first item, when the audience were applauding and the performers were taking their bow, Carina stole a glance at the front row.

Now she knew that her instinct had been right and the Duke was not engaged. Lady Virginia was not behaving like a woman who had made her conquest. There was a nervous determination in her manner that spoke of the hunter, still uncertain of her prey.

She simpered, she flirted, she laughed. But she could not hold his attention. That was fixed on Carina, his eyes glittering as he tried to penetrate her mask.

The performance continued, charming and proper. The gentlemen who had clapped and cheered the night before were looking glum. The women exchanged surprised glances, as if to say that if this was what their menfolk got up to when they were alone, then there was nothing to worry about.

At last it was time for Carina's solo. The others hurried off to change their costumes. She was aware of Bertie standing at the side, watching her intently.

When all was quiet, she began to sing. It was the song that she had written that afternoon from a full, aching heart.

The tune was based on the fragment of Chopin that she had played to the Duke at their first meeting, the one she had told him evoked happiness lost and past recall. She wondered if he would remember.

Softly, sweetly, she sang the words that were for him alone.

"How sweet the time we spent together,
How tenderly we loved each other.
But now the time has come to part,
Smiling face and broken heart.
Long and weary years stretch onward,
The shadowed road leads far away.
Will life give us one more meeting?
Who can say? Who can say?"

Her last note faded into nothing. There was a moment's total silence as the stunned audience seemed to awaken from the deep emotional experience that her song had aroused in them. Then there was loud and prolonged applause.

Carina was taken aback. Glancing to the side she saw Bertie, signalling for her to accept the applause. She rose uncertainly and curtsied.

There was more acclamation at the end of the whole performance. Everyone declared it a triumph, and the Duke ordered a footman to approach Bertie, while he himself left the room with Lady Virginia on his arm.

"His Grace desires you all to join him in the ballroom and take part in the dancing," the footman intoned.

Everyone beamed with delight. Carina felt her heart beat faster than usual.

They all entered the ballroom cautiously and were immediately summoned by the Duke, who was standing in the middle of a group of his society friends.

As well as Lady Virginia there was a large, middle-aged woman. She had a proprietorial manner and was rather over-dressed. Carina guessed that this was Lady Palmer.

"I am so glad to meet you all," she cried. "I said to my friend, the Duke, that there was really no reason why you should not join us. After all, you're not like common theatre people. Well, not exactly."

"Lilian – " The Duke laid his hand on her arm, endeavouring to restrain her, but she went on,

"In fact, I must say that you all look quite respectable."

"My friends are perfectly respectable," the Duke said with a tight smile. "Otherwise they would not be my friends."

Lady Virginia gave a rippling laugh.

"Oh, you're so right, David. I always say that you cannot choose your friends too carefully. And of course these dear, good people are the very best – well, the best of their kind."

The Duke signalled to footmen who hastily produced trays of glasses filled with champagne.

"I hope you all enjoy yourselves," he said with a touch of desperation.

Bertie handed a glass of champagne to Carina, and gently took her elbow.

"You know," he muttered as they drifted away, "high society people can be ruder than any others. Sometimes I wonder why I bother with them."

"You need their money," Carina said, smiling.

He sighed. "Lady Iris, how well you understand me. Ah, what a shame you can't stay with us! You and I would make a wonderful team."

"Yes, I think we would," she said wistfully.

"So come with us."

"I can't. It's been lovely but – well, I guess the time has come for me to return to my real life."

"But what do you mean your 'real' life? Who is to say which life is real and which isn't? Has it never occurred to you that the way you lived before might be no more than a preparation for your true destiny – as a *Bertie's Beauty*?"

She laughed outright at his suggestion.

"I love listening to you talk," she said. "Oh Bertie, it is such a delightful fantasy, but it can't come true."

"No, I suppose it can't," he said with a sigh. "You're too 'respectable'."

There was a gleam in his eyes that told her he was remembering Lady Palmer's *faux pas*.

"So are you," she said, taking up the joke. "Or at least, you *look* respectable."

"In fact," he said, "we neither of us look like 'common theatre people.'"

"We are *un*common theatre people," Carina agreed solemnly.

They burst out laughing together. Several people stared at them, and the Duke looked up from talking to Lady Virginia to give them a curious glance.

Bertie handed his empty glass to a footman and then did the same with Carina's glass.

"Dance with me, Lady Iris," he insisted.

"What about drumming up business?"

"To blazes with business! I may never get this chance again."

As she would have expected, he was a superb dancer and they twirled around the room in fine style. Soon everyone was watching them, evidently considering this part of the performance and when they had finished there was applause.

"Bertie, old friend," said the Duke, appearing behind him, "why don't you go and talk to Lord Mareham over there? He would like to hire you to perform at his house."

Bertie discreetly vanished and the Duke took Carina into his arms for the next waltz.

He held her indiscreetly close and she gasped at the feeling of being pressed against his powerful body.

"Your Grace," she protested, "think what people will say!"

"What do I care what people say?"

"And Lady Virginia?"

"So you've been listening to the gossip. Forget it. She will never be my bride, no matter what rumours her family spreads. I am an old hand at that game and very skilled at not being trapped."

His arms tightened around her even more.

"You mustn't do this," she murmured.

"Why not? You know that I want to hold you closer and closer yet. You do know that, don't you?"

"Yes," she said, half fainting with the storm of emotion within her.

"Do you know just how close I want to hold you?" he asked in a soft purposeful voice.

Carina felt herself blushing deeply at what she knew he meant. She forced herself to speak firmly.

"Your Grace, this is our last dance. I am here to say goodbye."

"Whatever do you mean?"

"We are leaving tonight. All of us."

"I know Bertie's going, but not you," he said firmly.

"I belong with the others."

"You belong with me."

The temptation to agree to anything he wanted was great, but she knew it must be resisted.

"You have your life and I have mine," she added breathlessly. "They will not touch again."

"The devil they won't. Didn't you hear me say that you belong to me?"

"Yes, I heard you say it," she said with a tiny flash of

temper, "but it is just not true. You don't own me just because you want me. In fact, you will never own me, because I will not be owned by any man. Not even by a Duke."

She knew she must try to cultivate her anger. It would give her the strength to leave him.

The music was coming to an end. Firmly Carina detached herself from him.

"You are a proud woman," he said admiringly. "I respect that, but it makes me more determined than ever to secure you for myself."

Lady Palmer came bustling towards them, calling his name. The Duke turned towards her, forcing a smile onto his face. Carina slipped away.

She made her way to the door and looked back at the Duke with wistful eyes. Then she fled.

*

"Well, that's that!" Bertie exclaimed, delighted. "The Duke has paid me handsomely and as soon as we've finished packing we shall be gone."

They were all in the little hallway that connected their rooms. Bertie was already in his outdoor clothes.

"I do wish we didn't have to go tonight," Julia said. "I need a good sleep first."

"So do we all, my dear," Bertie said. "But we have to reach London tomorrow, so we must collect Melanie at dawn. Everybody run and get ready now."

"I suppose Lady Iris will be staying here?" Helen drawled.

"Certainly not!" Carina said sharply. "I shall be travelling with you."

She realised that the others had probably been thinking the same as Helen, that she would remain at the castle to become the Duke's mistress. One or two of them were looking surprised at her firm declaration that this was not going to happen.

She would not allow herself to think of how much it would hurt to leave the Duke. She would pack and depart with the others. At her aunt's house they would collect Melanie and depart, while she remained.

She would never see the Duke again.

For a brief moment in time they had met as equals because her mystery intrigued him. Now he must return to his own world where he could marry Lady Virginia or some other grand lady.

And she would go back to her own dull little world, where everything would now remain grey.

If it were possible, she would try not to think of him.

But she knew it would not be possible.

Suddenly she was overwhelmed by the need to see him again, just one last time.

She slipped down the stairs and looked through the open door into the ballroom, but there was no sign of him.

She knew she must not stay here and risk discovery. But neither could she leave without one last glimpse.

Nearby there was a pair of French windows giving onto the garden. She could wait there for a few minutes. She opened the windows and stepped out.

The moon was out, flooding the garden with a magic blue light. Everything she saw filled her with wonder and delight. There was a profusion of flowers everywhere.

Then she noticed a large and beautiful fountain at the far end of the garden.

It was shining in the light from the moon and the stars. It was built of blue and white marble and it sparkled with colours as the water springing from the top poured down into a bowl which Carina was sure was at least two or three centuries old.

And the fountain was so beautiful that for a moment she could only stand and stare at it with delight.

"It is so lovely," she said aloud.

Then she jumped as a voice said,

"And so are you."

It was the Duke.

She was standing partly in the shadows and guessed he could not see her face too well. Perhaps he did not realise that she was no longer wearing a mask.

The moon shone on his face and she thought she saw a strange expression in his eyes which, for the moment, she could not understand.

"I came to say goodbye," she said.

"Do you really mean to leave me?" he asked quietly.

"I – I must."

"Do you feel nothing for me?"

"Do not ask me that," she begged.

He moved forward and stood looking down at her.

"You are not wearing your mask," he observed.

"No." Her lips barely moved.

She wondered if he would recognise her as the girl he had met years ago, on the night he was shot. Or perhaps the moonlight would make that harder. No recognition showed in his face as he gazed at her.

"You are very beautiful," he said fervently.

Then he put his arms around her and drew her closer to him. Almost before she realised what was happening, Carina felt his lips conquer hers.

As he drew her closer still, a strange feeling swept from her breast to her heart.

As the Duke's kiss held her captive, she thought for a moment she was flying up into the sky and touching the stars themselves.

He held her tighter and his kisses became more demanding so that she felt as if he was drawing her very heart from her body to make it his.

"So we reach the end of our games," he claimed huskily.

Carina tried to reply, but no words would come. Her heart was beating madly.

"Kiss me," he urged, caressing her lips again.

For a long time he held her clasped against him, while her heart soared.

"You are not leaving," he insisted.

"But I must – "

"No, you must not. You know that as well as I do. That is why you came out here. You wanted me to find you. You knew I would prevent you going."

"Did I?"

"Yes, because you know that what we have between us is too strong for both of us. You know that I cannot fight my passion for you, even if I wanted to. And I do not want to. You are mine, and I will never let you leave me again."

"You mean – ?" She hardly dared put her thoughts into words. Could he really mean what she desperately hoped? That he wanted to marry her?

"I mean that you and I must never part until the end of time. That song you sang tonight touched my soul. I recognised the tune. You wrote the words yourself, didn't you?"

"Yes, I did."

"And you meant them for me. You were warning me what life would be like without you, but I needed no

warning. There will be no *'smiling face and broken heart'*
for us. No *'long and weary years'* without each other. I will
not let you go. You are mine until the end of your days.
Promise me."

"I promise," she whispered.

"Swear it. Place your hand over your heart and vow to
give that heart to no other man as long as you shall live."

Solemnly she laid her hand over her heart.

"I swear it," she said. "No man but you, all my life."

He seized her hand and covered it with kisses.

"Bless you," he said fervently.

"And you?" she whispered. "Are you *mine*?"

"I think that no power on earth could take my heart
from you. Feel it."

He laid her hand over his breast, where she could feel
the soft beat of his heart.

"You hear me?" he said. "All yours, for ever."

"My love," she whispered, "my love – "

He kissed her again, her mouth, her eyes, her neck. He
almost seemed like a madman, covering her face with kisses.

"I shall smother you with jewels," he said hoarsely.
"Pearls, diamonds, sapphires, everything of the best. And
the world will wonder as you pass by."

His arms tightened, crushing her against him in
another powerful kiss. Now she could feel his heartbeat
again, not steady as last time, but wild, almost uncontrolled,
the heartbeat of a man driven to madness by his passion for
her.

Then he said, and his voice sounded strange,

"Go to bed, my darling. I will join you as soon as I can
get rid of the others."

"Wh – what?" she asked, not sure that she had heard

him properly.

"Go to your room. Get into bed and wait for me. I shall be with you quickly. Tonight we shall share a passion such as you have never known. Forget any other man who has ever loved you. When desire overwhelms us and you lie against my heart, no other man will exist."

White faced, she stared at him as his true meaning became plain.

"Don't look at me like that," he said softly. "I promise you that every word I say is true. Look."

He pulled something from his pocket and held it up. It was the most fabulous diamond bracelet Carina had ever seen. It must have cost a king's ransom.

"I was going to give you this when we were in bed tonight," he said, "but I can't wait."

He fixed it around her wrist. Carina stood thunderstruck, unable to speak or move or do anything to stop him.

"There," he said. "Now do you believe that I mean what I say?"

"Yes," she said hoarsely. "I believe you mean what you say."

"Tonight we will please each other in every way that is possible for a man and a woman. Tomorrow we will go abroad. I shall take you to Paris, Rome, Venice, anywhere you want. Now hurry and find Bertie, tell him that you are not going with him. Then go to bed and I will join you as soon as I can."

He turned and walked back inside, leaving Carina standing there in the moonlight, feeling as though her body and her heart had been turned to stone.

CHAPTER SEVEN

For a moment Carina could not move. Her heart was beating madly with anguish and a kind of panic.

What had just happened was so monstrous that she still could not quite believe it.

She loved him, and for a glorious moment she had thought he truly loved her and wanted to marry her.

But then the dream had died in the cruellest possible way.

He did not want to marry her. He planned to make her his mistress. Because in his eyes she was a common little showgirl, who could expect no better treatment.

As she turned to look once again at the fountain, she remembered what he had said.

"Forget any other man who has ever loved you."

He thought she had had a succession of lovers and was for sale to the highest bidder.

A sob rose to her throat. Turning she ran blindly back into the castle. Then she was hurrying quickly up the stairs to her bedroom. When she was safely inside, she flung herself down on the bed in a passion of weeping.

She loved him with her whole heart and soul, but he only desired her, while secretly despising her.

"It can't be true, it can't be true," she sobbed.

But she knew that it *was* true. The man, who had made

her vow never to give her heart to any other, had insulted her vilely only a moment later.

In a few minutes he planned to come to her bedroom, thinking that as a *Bertie's Beauty* she would know what was expected of her.

Because she was special, for the moment, he would shower her with jewels and take her abroad. But then they would return home and he would cast her off to marry a society lady.

And Carina was supposed to accept this as normal.

Her eye fell on the diamond bracelet. Beautiful and costly though it was, it seemed to her a badge of servitude. With a cry of horror she tore it off and hurled it across the room, buried her face in her hands again, weeping as though her heart would break.

If only she could bring herself to hate him!

But despite everything, she still loved him. She could not help herself. His kiss had been the most wonderful thing that had ever happened to her.

But to him she was just one of the girls who existed for the service of men, not only by what they said and how they acted, but because they gave men amusement and their bodies.

'I must get away,' she thought. 'I must go as quickly as possible.'

Pulling her case out of the cupboard, she started to pack all her belongings.

It did not take her long, because she had not brought a great deal with her.

She placed her mother's jewellery box carefully into her case and then she put on her ordinary dress and coat which she had worn when she had arrived at the castle.

When she was ready, she looked around the room to

see if she had left anything behind.

Then she knew that there was one thing still to be done.

There was a pen and writing paper on the dressing table. Sitting down she hurriedly began to write.

She wrote only a few words and they did not really satisfy her, but they came from her heart. She folded the paper and put it into an envelope, but did not address it.

She retrieved the bracelet from the corner where she had flung it and put that into the envelope too.

Then she laid it on her pillow and quickly left the room.

She had written,

Forgive me. It could never be.

Your Iris.

Downstairs she found the three carriages in which the troupe had arrived were almost ready to go. The last of the luggage was being piled in.

"There you are," Bertie exclaimed, relieved to see her. "In you get."

Carina climbed into the first carriage without a word, hoping that he would not see the suffering on her face. A few minutes later they were rumbling out of the castle gates.

*

After the Duke had left Carina, he hurried into the ballroom. His feverish mind was full of the thought of her waiting for him in her room. With all his soul he longed to go to her at once, but he knew that he still had a duty to his guests.

The band from the village was playing vigorously and with a good deal of skill.

The room was full of beautiful women in gorgeous

clothes. Many of them were society ladies, the kind he had known all his life. He was at ease with them. Normally he enjoyed their company.

Now he barely noticed them, although they smiled and waved at him and he waved back, but only mechanically.

His mind was on Lady Iris and the love they would soon share.

'I don't even know her real name,' he mused. 'And yet she fills my mind and heart.'

He looked round and saw Lady Palmer at the far end of the room. He joined her and she said, simpering,

"Why David, wherever have you been? We've all been wondering and I know one young lady who's been wondering more than most."

With a slight nod she indicated Lady Virginia, waltzing by with Viscount Manton. She contrived to smile at the Duke over her partner's shoulder.

He smiled back, but in fact he was suddenly full of weariness. He was so tired of it all, the endless society machinations, the girls smiling at him because they wanted to be a Duchess.

Worst of all were the girls who docilely agreed with every word he said. He much preferred Lady Iris who teased and contradicted him, challenged him to his face and then vanished with a laugh.

Until tonight, when she had not vanished. Tonight she was waiting for him upstairs in her bed.

Inwardly he groaned, thinking how long he must wait. The kiss he had stolen from her had been more wonderful than any kiss he could ever remember. Her lips had been soft and warm, full of invitation.

In a colourful life, he had kissed a great number of women and had often thought himself in love.

Too many times. And the love had always been fleeting.

As a young man he had been wild, amusing himself with bored wives and there were many of them.

Ladies who had married men for their titles, respectable matrons whose husbands spent their time gambling or drinking, women married to faithless husbands. All of them opened their arms eagerly to the handsome young man whose only object was to enjoy himself and who had plenty of money to spend.

They had all been women of experience who had understood only too well the game they were playing.

Only once had things gone wrong and that had nearly cost him his life. An angel had come to rescue him. And then she had vanished, never to be seen again.

That was probably a good thing. She had been young and innocent and by now was probably a sedate wife and mother, with a large waist and a brood of children. And only he would ever remember that she had once been an angel.

For some reason that he could not understand, he had thought of her a lot recently. Now he had a mysterious feeling of loss, as though he were about to say a final goodbye to her.

He tried to shrug the thought aside. Tonight only Iris mattered. When he had seen her face earlier, he had been struck by her beauty. But the moonlight had smoothed out details and he still had only a vague idea of how she looked.

But when he visited her bedroom tonight, he would know for sure. The passion he had felt when their lips touched was something he had never experienced before. But he was determined to experience it again.

He had said that she belonged to him and now, more than ever, he knew that it must be true.

As the evening progressed, it was with the greatest

difficulty that the Duke stopped himself from urging people to leave. He was longing to be rid of them, so that he could be alone with his Lady Iris.

'I must be mad,' he said to himself. 'After all, I hardly know her. Yet I feel as if she is drawing me towards her and I long to respond.'

The ball seemed to drag on interminably. He wondered if Lady Iris might simply go to sleep and not be pleased to see him when he did appear.

At last his impatience got the better of him. Smiling but determined, he finally told Lady Palmer that it was too late for them to dance any longer and he thought after the next dance, the band should play 'God Save The Queen'.

"Oh, must we go?" she enquired. "It is so lovely being here."

"I am glad you are enjoying it," he replied untruthfully. "But it has been a long day."

He started to say goodnight to the older people who were leaving.

The younger ones, although some of them must have been very tired after the races, were still dancing around the room.

When finally the band broke into the National Anthem, they were obviously disappointed they had to stop dancing.

Now the Duke began to urge them to depart, finding it difficult to move those who, when the dancing stopped, had hurried once more to the delicious refreshments in the room next door.

Glancing at the clock he realised that it was already two o'clock in the morning.

Finally the last guest had left. The Duke hurried away leaving the servants clearing up. Still wearing his evening clothes, he ran upstairs to Carina's bedroom.

The lights in the passage had been turned out as was usual. But he found it easy to make his way, because the moon was full and the curtains were not completely drawn over the windows.

He knew which bedroom was hers, because he had seen her looking from the window the night before. It was a corner room, the best in that part of the castle.

He opened the door and found the room in complete darkness.

She must be asleep, he thought, trying to listen for her breathing.

For a moment he hesitated.

Perhaps he should leave her to sleep.

But then he knew that it was impossible for him to turn away.

Fortunately he had some matches in his pocket, because he had smoked while he was watching Bertie's theatrical performance.

Vaguely, in the light coming from the corridor, he could make out the dressing-table.

He made his way towards it. Drawing out his matches he lit two candles. Then he turned round to look towards the huge four-poster bed.

There was no one there.

To his astonishment he saw that the bed had not been slept in.

For a moment he thought he must be in the wrong room.

But then, looking around the room by the light of the candle, he saw that the doors of the cupboards were open and that the chest of drawers had been emptied.

Was it possible that Iris had run away from him?

His mind rejected it. Her passion for him had been as great as his for her. He knew he could not be mistaken about that. When he had held her against him he had known the truth.

And yet now she wished to deny that truth.

Then he saw the envelope on the pillow. It bore no name but he knew it was meant for himself. He snatched it up and tore it open and at once the bracelet fell out.

He frowned. What woman could bring herself to reject so much and the promise of more to come?

But perhaps she was holding out for higher terms. He made a wry face. Somehow he had thought her better than that, but in the end he supposed they were all the same.

But then he read the few words in the letter.

Forgive me, but it could never be.

Your Iris.

Somehow the very simplicity of the words convinced him.

She had gone, deserting him so completely that she had even refused his fabulous gift.

And in the same breath she had called herself '*your Iris*'.

She was his. She had said so.

And then she had left him.

For the first time a twinge of doubt assailed him.

"But she cannot have gone far," he thought. "Bertie will know."

Going downstairs he summoned his housekeeper and asked whether *Bertie's Beauties* had departed yet.

"Oh yes, Your Grace," she said. "An hour ago."

"And they all left?" he asked. "Did none of them remain behind?"

"I didn't actually see them go, Your Grace."

The answer was supplied by a footman who had watched everyone climb aboard and could swear that everybody had gone.

"Did Bertie say where he was going?" the Duke demanded.

"London, Your Grace," the footman said triumphantly. "A telegram arrived for him this afternoon, summoning him to London to the purposes of employment."

"But where? Where?" the Duke asked, in agony.

"That he did not say, Your Grace."

"Never mind. London is helpful. Those three carriages cannot travel very fast. A swift horse should overtake them on the London road, even with an hour's headstart. Send a message to the stables. I want my fastest horse ready in ten minutes."

In less than ten minutes he was in the stables, dressed for riding. When his speediest horse was led out, he mounted in one leap and in a moment was galloping out of the yard.

He rode all through the night, always expecting to overtake the three carriages at any moment. But there was no sign of them.

It was as though *Bertie's Beauties* had vanished into thin air, taking Lady Iris with them.

*

Bertie and his troupe had travelled only four miles on the London road, before turning off onto the lane that led to the village of Tremingham, just beyond which lay the home of Carina's aunt.

To her relief the others in the carriage, Julia, Bertie and Samson, all dozed throughout the journey, so there was nobody to see her misery. Carina sat in the corner, her face turned to the window while tears streamed down her face.

At last she could cry no longer and stared out at the world, despairingly watching the first cold light of dawn appear.

By the time they were drawing up to her aunt's house, the day had begun.

"I wonder how Melanie is," Bertie mused. "I do hope she has improved."

Receiving no answer he turned his head to where Carina was staring out of the window, a look of consternation on her face.

"What's the matter?" he asked.

"It's my aunt," Carina said in a tense voice. "She's come home. There she is now, standing at the window."

Bertie glanced to where she was pointing and saw a woman who stood watching their arrival with a grim look on her face.

"She looks very disapproving," he muttered. "I'm afraid she's heard the worst."

"What worst?" Carina demanded. "Even the very worst isn't too bad."

"Then she's been told another worst that is very bad," Bertie said. "Oh dear! I hope she hasn't murdered Melanie and disposed of her body under the floorboards."

"Bertie, that's my aunt you're talking about. She is a very kind, reasonable lady."

"Are you sure? Right now she looks as though she'd like to drink my blood!"

"You are wrong."

"And when she's finished with me, she'll move onto you. Mind you, she would make a wonderful Lady Macbeth."

Carina sighed and gave up. Bertie, in this mood, was

incorrigible. Besides, Aunt Mary did look very grim. Anyone who did not know her well, she thought, might not realise what a nice, understanding person she really was.

Just the same, Carina would have preferred not to have her discover the whole story in this way.

The others in the two rear carriages were looking out of the windows. Bertie jumped down and shouted to them urgently not to get out.

"Turn the carriages round and be ready for a quick getaway," he ordered.

"Bertie!" Carina urged, exasperated. "Come on, it's not as bad as that."

"We'll see," he told her darkly.

Together they approached the door, which was already being pulled open by Jennings. His eyes, fixed on Carina, said helplessly that none of this was his fault.

As they entered the hall, Aunt Mary emerged and advanced on Bertie.

"Good morning," she said coldly. "You, I take it, are Mr. – ?"

"I am Bertie, at your service, madam," he said, greeting her with a theatrical bow.

"Mr. Bertie, I suppose I should thank you for restoring my niece to me, however ill-advised it was of you to take her away in the first place. And however ill-advised it was of her to go with you."

"Aunt – "

"I will speak to you in a moment, miss."

Carina gasped. She had never known her aunt in this mood. Bertie had been right.

He pulled himself together.

"I am indebted to Miss Denton," he said, "for her kindness in rescuing my friends and myself from the most unfortunate accident that befell us here a couple of days ago. Perhaps you have not heard – "

"I have spoken to Miss Melanie Carlyle, to whom, of course, I am glad to extend hospitality," Aunt Mary broke in. "That is not the issue."

"I was afraid it might not be," Bertie muttered gloomily.

"The issue, sir, is that my niece, a gently reared girl, was induced to visit a den of iniquity in your company."

"But not my company alone," Bertie protested. "There were also the three other young ladies."

If he thought this would help matters he was soon disillusioned.

"I prefer," Aunt Mary said stiffly, "not to speak of the kind of 'young lady' who joins a singing and dancing troupe, flaunting their bodies for the dubious pleasure of men. I take it the audience was entirely male."

"But you are mistaken dear lady," Bertie said fervently. "Why last night Lady Palmer herself – "

"I am talking about the night before," Aunt Mary insisted. "The county is buzzing with tales of a lewd and disgusting performance, at which no true lady would be present, let alone take part in."

"It was not lewd and disgusting," Carina said indignantly. "Some of the songs were a little bit – well, just a little bit – "

With her aunt's gimlet eye on her Carina, wished she had never started to speak.

A welcome diversion was provided by the entrance of Melanie.

Bertie greeted her enthusiastically and she hugged him back. Then she hugged Carina. She was looking better, but Carina wondered if her arm was really strong enough to play the piano.

"I saw you arriving from my room and started packing at once," she said.

"Are you well enough to come with us?" Bertie asked.

"Oh yes, I do so want to be back with the others. Mrs. Jensen has been very kind," she gave Aunt Mary a shy look, "but I do not wish to impose on her any more."

"Then I will give my grateful thanks to Mrs. Jenson, and depart," Bertie said.

He turned to Carina taking her hand in his. "Lady Iris – that is – "

"It's all right, Bertie dear," she said softly. "I will be all right."

"Are you sure?"

He rolled his eyes in Aunt Mary's direction.

"Of course I am sure," she said urgently.

She was certain that when he had gone, her aunt would thaw.

"Then we'll be off. Why don't you see us to the door?"

Carina walked out into the hall with them. Melanie quickly kissed her cheek before hurrying out and jumping into one of the carriages.

Bertie dropped his voice.

"I just want you to know that there'll always be a place for you in *Bertie's Beauties*. Always."

"Thank you Bertie, dear. It was a wonderful time but – " she sighed, "it is something that will never happen again. And don't worry about my aunt. She's not really as fierce as all that."

They hugged each other. Then he ran to climb aboard and the next moment the three carriages were rumbling away.

Carina had spoken more confidently than she felt. She had never seen her aunt in this mood.

But when she returned to the drawing room, she found Aunt Mary looking as stern as before.

"And now," she demanded, "I want you to tell me what happened."

"Aunt, I don't understand. You were going to see your sister-in-law – "

"My sister-in-law," replied Aunt Mary acidly, "exaggerated her condition like the hypochondriac that she is. When I realised the truth I gave her my private opinion, we quarrelled and I left the house.

"I arrived home last night to find the countryside agog with the story of your exploits. It seems that my departure was the signal for an orgy of dissipation."

"It wasn't – "

"Before I left I warned you that the Duke of Westbury was a man whom a respectable young woman should avoid. And within a few hours you were in his home, disporting yourself for the pleasure of men."

"I wore a mask," Carina protested. "Nobody could have known my identity."

"Everyone knows. You were seen driving off from this house with *Bertie's Beauties*, or whatever silly name they call themselves. Servants talk. And why wear a mask, unless you knew you were doing wrong?"

"Doing wrong?" Carina echoed sadly.

It seemed a terrible way to describe her blazing moments of joy with the man who had won her love. But he had tried to make her his mistress and had believed she would find it acceptable.

So perhaps her aunt was right and she had done

wrong?

That was the cruellest and most heart-breaking moment that she had endured.

"I am seriously disappointed in you," Aunt Mary resumed. "As you know, I was hoping to introduce you into local society and perhaps help you to meet a man who might marry you. However, that is now out of the question. Your reputation is – well – "

"You mean my reputation is besmirched," Carina said bitterly.

"Unfortunately, that is true. I suggest you return quietly to your own home and remain there."

So that was her future, she thought. Banished to the country to live in perpetual isolation as though no decent person would associate with her.

It was as though a flash of lightning had lit up her world, illuminating two lives – the dreary one that could so easily swallow her up, and the other one, glittering, glamorous and exciting, that could be hers if only she had the courage.

Suddenly Carina found that she was moving. She was not aware of making a decision, but her limbs seemed to go into action of their own accord.

With one hand she seized her cloak, which she had thrown down on a chair. With another hand she snatched up her bag.

Then she was racing out into the hall. Jennings, who had been eavesdropping, started up. Then, reading intent in her face, he pulled open the door.

In a moment she was out of the house and flying down the path, calling,

"Bertie, Bertie! Wait for me! I'm coming. *I'm coming!*"

CHAPTER EIGHT

Bond Street in London was where the fashionable bride went to choose her wedding gifts and the day after she became engaged, Lady Virginia Chesterham could be seen browsing, arm in arm with her future husband.

She wasted no time embarking on this expedition, because, as her mother had said to her,

"You are not getting any younger, my dear, and the sooner your marriage takes place the better."

Aspreys was her destination. Here there were truly costly gifts to be found, such as befitted a titled lady.

The huge silver epergne was almost the most expensive item in the shop. So of course, the Duke thought wryly, Lady Virginia would be sure to want it.

He stood watching with sardonic amusement as she cooed over it, finally raising shining eyes to his.

"Is that really what you want?" he asked.

"Oh yes, yes, it's the most beautiful thing I have ever seen. It will look just perfect in the middle of the dining table and everyone will admire it."

The Duke signalled to the assistant who eagerly began work on the paperwork.

Lady Virginia clasped her hands under her chin in an affectation of pleasure.

"Oh, thank you! Thank you!"

"My dear," the Duke replied languidly. "Think nothing of it."

"Oh, but I must."

She reached out, clasping his hands in both hers.

"So generous," she said, gazing radiantly up into his face.

Unseen by either of them, the figure of a young woman appeared in the doorway. She had been window-shopping, but the sight of a familiar male figure inside had brought her a few steps further forward, to see if it was really him.

And if it should be him, what harm could it do to watch him, just for a moment? It was four weeks since they had parted and her heart yearned for just a glimpse.

So she moved closer and saw that it really was the man she loved. For a moment she stood quite still, possessed by a bittersweet feeling that shook her to the soul.

Surely she could attract his attention, just for a moment? She would be strong and go away afterwards, but just a word, a look –

But then she saw another figure that she recognised. Lady Virginia Chesterham seized the Duke's hands in hers, gazing up into his face with her most dazzling smile.

Carina, standing like stone, could not hear what she said, but she saw the Duke smiling down on her.

"Can I help you, madam?" an assistant asked her.

"Thank you, no – I am sure things are much too expensive for me."

"Well, we do sell to the highest titles in the land," he said gently.

"Like Lady Virginia?" Carina asked.

"You know her?"

"Not exactly – "

"It is always nice when a bridal couple comes here," he enthused.

"A bridal – ?"

"Lady Virginia's wedding will be the event of the London season. St. George's, Hanover Square, and then Rome for the honeymoon. And so many of the wedding gifts have been chosen here. If you know her, would you like to – ?"

"Oh no, thank you. She wouldn't remember me."

'And he,' she thought sadly, 'would show no sign of remembering me. And perhaps he would *not* remember me at all"

"Thank you," she said hurriedly. Slipping out of the door she ran down the street, desperate to escape before the man she loved could recognise her.

*

There were some things that a bridal couple did not say to each other, because they were unnecessary.

Viscount Manton would never mention to his betrothed that just before she had accepted him, she had been angling furiously to snare the Duke of Westbury.

Lady Virginia, in her turn, would never say bluntly that it was only the realisation that the Duke had slipped beyond her grasp that had made her finally turn to a man whose title was inferior to her father's.

The daughter of an Earl did not marry a mere Viscount, unless she was desperate.

But Lady Virginia *was* desperate. Having set her sights on the Duke she had spurned other suitors while valuable time had passed by. She was now twenty-five years old and ready to settle for what she could secure.

And the best she could find was Viscount Manton, who had adored her hopelessly for years. He knew that his bride did not love him, but he too was ready to settle for what he could get.

Likewise, neither of the two men could admit to each other that the lady was marrying the 'wrong' one because she could not win the other.

Instead, the three of them must perform a stately dance, confirming their roles of adoring couple and devoted family friend.

It was in the service of this dance that the Duke had accompanied them to Aspreys, so that the three of them might choose his wedding gift.

"So generous," she repeated now, her eyes fixed on the Duke's face. "You're the dearest of friends to both of us. Giles, isn't he our very best friend?"

"Certainly," the Viscount agreed, turning away from where he had been examining jewellery. "Although a really good friend would have agreed to be my best man."

"No, no, I want the Duke to give me away," Lady Virginia asserted. "Since my dear Papa is an invalid, there is no one more suitable than the Duke, who has always been a second father to me."

"Thank you," he said, wryly appreciating these tactics. "You are very kind, both of you, but I regret I shall be abroad. Now, Lady Virginia, is there anything else I can tempt you with?"

"Lady Virginia?" she pouted, adding softly, "You used to call me Virginia."

"That was before you became another man's fiancée," he observed. "How about some jewellery? That is, if your betrothed doesn't mind."

"Oh, he won't mind whatever you buy me. He says he wants me to have absolutely anything I want."

"In that case, go and choose some diamonds."

As he had hoped, this distracted her predatory mind.

While she was surveying necklaces, the Viscount drew closer to his friend and asked,

"You still haven't found her?"

"Not a sign of her. Not a hint, not a whisper. I was so sure I would pass Bertie's carriages on the London road. They couldn't have travelled fast enough to elude me, but they vanished into nothing.

"Since coming to London I can find no trace. I have been to the place where Bertie used to live, but he's gone."

"And even if you found Bertie, would she be with him?" the Viscount asked. "When they were performing for us at Westbury Castle, I seem to remember somebody saying that Iris was a last minute addition, filling in for someone else."

"Yes, so do I, but I didn't think to ask further," the Duke said. "Why should I? I was so sure that no woman I wanted would ever leave me. Even when she challenged me and warned me that she wasn't like the others, I did not heed her warning.

"In fact I didn't heed it until she was gone, and I was sitting there like a fool, holding the thousand pound diamond bracelet she had tossed back at me as though it was a tinker's bauble."

"I hope you got your money back," the Viscount said prosaically.

"No, I still have the bracelet. It gives me hope that one day I will meet her again and put the past right."

"But if she is so determined to avoid you – "

"That is what fills me with dread. And yet, sometimes I seem to feel her near me. When I turn she's never actually there, but she haunts my dreams and my waking hours until I think perhaps I am going mad."

He gave a brief laugh. "Can a man be haunted by a living woman? I certainly am."

"My dear fellow," the Viscount said, genuinely concerned. "You are not yourself."

"No, I am no longer myself, but when I think of the arrogant creature I used to be, I'm glad. If I met her now, I could tell her that she has made me a better man."

"Then you will find her again," his friend declared.

"I do wish I could believe so."

A brittle giggle from Lady Virginia made them turn.

"Oh, do look," she said, holding up a diamond necklace. "Isn't this too divine?"

"Exquisite," the Duke said, forcing a smile.

"And there's this as well," she said, reaching onto the counter for another glittering diamond piece and holding it up.

"Such a lovely bracelet to go with it," she sighed.

"No!"

The shout came suddenly from the Duke before he could stop himself. He pulled himself together quickly.

"I was mistaken," he said shakily. "Diamonds do not suit you. You should only wear pearls. Their soft glow is just right for you."

They settled on a pearl tiara and the Duke generously added a matching pearl tie pin for the Viscount.

"My best wishes to you both," he said hurriedly. "I wish you a long and happy life together."

There was another thing the Duke could not say about the lady to her fiancé.

That he was glad to be rid of her.

*

Mrs. Babbage's boarding house was in one of the

117

poorer parts of London and its aspect was definitely shabby. But inside it was warm and clean and *Bertie's Beauties* were made to feel comfortable.

Comfortable but not happy. The employment they had hurried back to London to obtain had not been forthcoming, for reasons that still caused friction.

"Herbert was supposed to be a friend of yours," Julia observed, not for the first time, as she lolled discontentedly on the sofa in their communal room.

"He *was* a friend of mine," said Bertie, also not for the first time, "Until he behaved in a way that I found unacceptable."

"You mean he made advances to Carina," Samson chipped in.

"Yes," Bertie said, "and since she's new to this life, I felt it necessary to protect her."

"Couldn't you have protected Carina without throwing him down the stairs?" James demanded gloomily.

"I agree that was a little extreme," Bertie admitted self-consciously.

"And unnecessary," Samson pointed out. "I would have been glad to have done it for you."

Bertie considered this suggestion, then shook his head.

"No, you would have overdone it."

"Overdone it?" Helen squealed. "You broke his wrist."

"His wrist was not broken," Bertie corrected her with dignity. "Merely sprained."

"Broken or sprained," she shot back, "he *still* said he wouldn't employ us if we were the last act on earth. We *still* don't have an engagement. You *still* had to move out of your rooms because they were too expensive. We *still* – "

"Yes, yes I take your point," Bertie interrupted hastily.

"My point is that all our misfortunes are due to Carina," Helen declared bitterly. "Nothing went wrong before she joined us, but since then, nothing has gone right."

"That is not true," Bertie said, flaring into one of his rare tempers. "You shouldn't say things like that about her."

The others glared at Helen. Everyone knew that it was madness to challenge Bertie about Carina. He was completely unreasonable on the subject.

"Oh, you always defend her," Helen said with a shrug.

"Of course I do," Bertie said at once. "You know that Melanie's arm has been very slow to recover, and I doubt if she will ever be able to play the piano as she used to.

"Not that it makes any difference. That handsome young doctor she saw when we reached London was definitely making eyes at her. I think he'll be deciding her future. So where would we be without Carina?"

"No worse off, since without an engagement we can't perform anyway," Helen pointed out with unanswerable logic.

"But we might get an engagement soon," Bertie insisted.

"Not while you assault people," Samson added.

Bertie glared at him.

"I do not assault 'people'," he said, "merely Herbert, because he deserved it. And you are wrong about Carina. The fact is – " he stopped, looking embarrassed.

"What?" they all wanted to know.

"She knows how bad our financial situation is and – well, if you must know, she's selling some of her jewellery to help us. That's where she has gone today, to the West End."

There was silence.

"Is that true?" Helen asked sceptically.

"Perfectly true. In fact, I am not supposed to tell you. Carina didn't want anyone else to know. But those jewels she wore when we performed at Westbury Castle – the tiara and ear-rings – they are genuine. They belonged to her mother. Now she's selling them to help us."

Another silence, this time a shocked one.

"You shouldn't have let her do that," James said.

"I couldn't stop her," Bertie defended himself. "She's headstrong when she makes her mind up. And she, too, blames herself for that engagement we lost."

He looked at the clock.

"She ought to be back by now," he said worriedly. "I wish she had not gone alone. And before anyone blames me for that, she insisted on it."

"I think that is her now," Anthony said, looking out of the window at the road.

Bertie hurried out quickly and was in time to help Carina down from the hansom cab.

"You look pale," he said. "Did you have a bad time? Oh, I should never have let you go alone."

"No, I was all right," Carina replied in a low voice.

She paid the cab driver and hurried inside. In the hall she stopped and pressed something into Bertie's hand.

"Here is all the money I raised," she said. "It should take care of us all for a while."

"Bless you," he said. "Come in and have some tea with the rest of us."

"No, I'll just go upstairs, I think. I have a headache."

"You are ill," he said, taking her hands in his.

"No, I'm just – I had a shock, that's all. I will be all right."

She tore her hands from his and ran up the stairs lest

he see that she was crying.

Bertie stood at the bottom of the stairs, looking at the money that she had given him and listening to the closing of her door above his head. He was deeply troubled.

He went to find Mrs. Babbage and paid her all the rent that was owed. Beaming, she said that tea would be ready at any moment.

A few minutes later he climbed the stairs and stopped outside Carina's room. From inside he could hear the sound of desperate sobbing. It hurt him to the heart.

At last he knocked, very softly. But there was no response. Only more terrible heart-broken sobs.

He knocked again, and when there was still no answer, Bertie gingerly opened the door and looked in.

As he had feared, Carina was stretched out on her bed, weeping into her pillow. Her whole body shook with grief and Bertie stared, aghast.

"Carina," he started tenderly.

She coughed and then struggled to sit up, groping for her handkerchief.

"I am sorry to intrude on you like this," he said humbly. "I wouldn't offend you for the world, you know that. I will go away if you tell me to, but I hope you don't. I would rather stay and help you."

"Thank you, Bertie dear," she said in a choking voice. "But nobody can help me."

"Did something happen while you were out today?"

"I saw him," she said directly.

"Him?"

"The Duke. I know I should have put him out of my mind, but it was very silly of me, you see. I thought he really loved me. But just before we left the castle he – well, he just thought of me as a mistress."

"He tried to make you his mistress?" Bertie breathed in horror.

"Oh, yes. He promised to shower me with jewels and take me abroad, but I didn't care about that. All I wanted was for him to love me. And he doesn't, not really."

"I think he must do," Bertie said sadly. "Because no man could know you and not love you."

Carina raised her eyes to him, wondering if he had really meant what he had said, but Bertie had hurriedly changed the subject.

"Look, I've brought you some tea," he said. "Sit up properly and drink it, there's a good girl."

His fatherly tone soothed her. She forced herself to sit up straight and sip the tea, which tasted good.

"Did you speak to him today?" Bertie asked.

"Oh no, he was with his – his – fiancée."

"His *fiancée?*"

"Lady Virginia. We saw her at the castle. Everyone said that they would marry, and now it's settled. They were in Aspreys in Bond Street. I saw them together, holding hands, and one of the assistants told me about them. He said their wedding will be the event of the season."

"After all the things he said to you?" Bertie demanded.

"It is not the same," Carina murmured sadly. "He never thought of marrying me. I believe he forgot me the day after I left. And now I, too, will forget him. I will, I *will.*"

Her control broke and she flung herself back down on the bed. Her misery and the fierceness in her voice when she said those last words, told everything about the depth of her love.

Bertie bent his head.

*

Carina's sacrifice of her jewellery seemed to mark a turning point, for almost at once the troupe's fortunes changed.

Every day Bertie haunted the offices of theatrical producers and theatre owners and at last he met someone he had known in his early acting days, and who greeted him like a long lost brother.

"His name is Stanley Bentiss," he told everyone that evening. He has taken the Majestic Theatre for a production of *Twelfth Night.*

"He belongs to the old school of producers, the kind who like to give the audience full value for their money, so as well as the play he wants us to perform."

"But when?" Julia wanted to know.

"We appear at the start, then we come on again during each of the two intervals. But we also appear *during* the play."

"I've read *Twelfth Night,*" Helen observed.

"It doesn't say anything about *Bertie's Beauties.*"

"But it does say *'if music be the food of love, play on'*," Bertie riposted. "We shall prove that it *is* the food of love, by performing for Count Orsino, and later at Olivia's court. We will also sing and dance at the wedding festivities at the end."

"I don't think that's quite what Shakespeare envisaged," Samson pronounced. "In fact he would probably object strongly."

"Then it's lucky he's dead," Bertie added with spirit. "Besides, it's done all the time."

Carina knew that he was quite right. Most modern interpretations of Shakespeare contained the same kind of cavalier treatment. But she, too, had trouble envisaging *Bertie's Beauties* in this setting.

But still, it was work, in a major theatre and she congratulated Bertie.

"Actually," he said, becoming self-conscious, "there *is* something else."

They clamoured for him to tell them.

"I told you Stanley knew me as an actor. He saw me play Feste in this very play and – " he finished with a modest shrug.

"And he wants you to play the part," Carina exclaimed.

"That's right. The extra money will help me pay back what I owe you. Things are looking up, my children. We are going to be rich at last."

In his excitement he jumped up and began to stride around the room. His pacing took him to the window, where he stopped, as if thunderstruck.

"What is it, Bertie?" Carina asked, coming to stand beside him.

Then she too froze as she saw the Duke climbing out of a hansom cab.

"Oh, no! He mustn't find me here. I can't ever see or speak to him again. Please Bertie, please help me!" she pleaded.

"Go upstairs," he said in a strange voice. "We'll protect you."

She fled. At the top of the stairs she looked down and saw Mrs. Babbage open the front door and admit a tall figure that she could so easily recognise, even from this height.

Slowly she backed into her own room and shut the door, burying her face in her hands.

Down below, the Duke strode into the sitting room, smiling when he saw Bertie, holding out his hand.

"Bertie, my old friend," he exclaimed. "It's taken me

so long to find you."

"Your Grace!" Bertie took the outstretched hand with a reasonable show of cordiality. "I had not hoped to see you again so soon."

"Yes, you vanished so suddenly I almost thought you were escaping me. I went to your old address, but they said you had left."

"Those rooms were very expensive, and I had to seek somewhere cheaper, as you see. How did you find us?"

"My man saw you in the street today. Knowing that I was seeking you, he followed you here and then hurried to my house to tell me."

He looked around at the others, regarding him silently.

"Bertie may I speak with you alone?"

Bertie gave a brief nod and the others slipped away.

"I want to speak to you man to man," the Duke said when the door had closed. "It is about that young woman who came to the castle with you. You called her Lady Iris, but I never knew her real name."

"I didn't know it myself," Bertie said, straight-faced.

"You must know it. How did you meet her?"

"Through the road accident when our regular pianist was injured. She was in the other carriage, and volunteered to help. We took Melanie to a nearby hotel and our new friend came to the castle with us.

"She chose to go by the name of Iris, fearful that the occupation she was about to enter was not very proper for a respectable lady. For she *is* a lady you know, educated and refined. It was natural that she should wish to conceal her true identity."

"Of course she is a lady," the Duke growled. "You do not have to tell me that."

"I thought there might have been some

misunderstanding on the point."

"No misunderstanding," the Duke replied in the same harsh voice.

"You will understand, then, that certain things are not possible for her."

"Just tell me where she is."

"But I don't know."

"Nonsense, she left with you."

"Initially, yes. But she stayed with me only while we did a detour to collect Melanie."

"That's why I couldn't find you on the London road."

"Probably. At any rate, she's gone."

"But where, man, where?"

"That I couldn't say."

"Damn! I was sure I would find her with you." The Duke's face was livid. "How can I have come so close, only to lose her now?"

"Perhaps it was never meant to be," Bertie said gravely.

"I will not believe that. I have to find her."

"But perhaps she does not want to be found," Bertie suggested. "Why did she leave you, sir?"

"That – I cannot tell you. I only know that she loves me as I love her."

"But if she was convinced of your love, your true and honest love, why would she abandon you?" Bertie asked, and his voice held a touch of sternness that stunned the Duke.

Whirling, he faced Bertie, eyes narrowing.

"Are you daring to judge me?" he demanded arrogantly.

"Have you done anything for which you should be judged?" Bertie asked. "Ask yourself that honestly."

He knew he must be going mad. To alienate a valuable patron was a form of insanity. But nothing mattered now but Carina, her grief, and his own chance to save her from this cruel man, who came in search of her, despite being practically married.

"I will say this just once more," the Duke told him coldly. "If you know where Lady Iris is, I insist that you tell me. Do not argue with me or question me. I owe you no explanations."

"Nor I you, Your Grace," Bertie said quietly.

"Tell me how to find her."

Bertie faced him squarely.

"I cannot do that. I don't know where she is or what she is called. I last saw her on the day we left the castle."

The two men faced each other, both hard-eyed and each in his own way, determined.

"Give up, Your Grace," Bertie said. "You've lost her. Perhaps you threw her away. And some things, once lost, can never be reclaimed."

That answer seemed to do what nothing else could. The hard light died from the Duke's eyes and his shoulders sagged, as though he was overtaken by defeat.

"You are right," he said, and walked out without another word.

Bertie waited until the cab had drawn away from the door before he went upstairs and found Carina.

"Has he gone?" she asked huskily.

"Yes, he's gone. Don't cry. It's all over. I promise you need never see him again. There, there, my dearest, don't cry. Don't cry."

CHAPTER NINE

Carina had not wasted her time since joining the troupe. During the weeks when they had languished at Mrs. Babbage's, she had taken over the battered piano in the parlour and discovered in herself a gift for song writing.

She had begun to realise her potential during the two days she had spent at the castle. Now she had time to bring it to fruition and she gloried in the development of her talent.

By the time the troupe was ready to start rehearsals for *Twelfth Night* she had composed a collection of new songs, which Bertie fell on with joy.

"This one to open with," he said, "and this one to sing for Orsino – "

"I have written some music for Feste's songs, too," she said. "But perhaps Mr. Bentiss has already commissioned that music from someone else?"

But it turned out that Stanley Bentiss was indeed expecting the music from Bertie. He was so pleased with Carina's offering that he made a separate payment to her for all the music in the play.

A very strange feeling came over her as she looked at the money, the first she had ever earned.

"I don't believe it," she murmured.

"You must believe it," Bertie said. "You have a great talent, great enough to earn you a living."

In the world Carina came from a lady was not expected to earn a living. Now she felt an immense sense of pride and a smile spread over her face. Bertie saw it and was delighted.

"That's it," he said. "You really do belong in this life."

It seemed as though she did. The knowledge helped to blur the memory of her other life.

Sometimes she would lie awake at night, not thinking about the Duke, just feeling, and hoping that one day the ache in her heart would go away.

She could see his face as it had been in their last moments together, full of ardour, speaking words of passion. At these times it was hard not to weep, but she managed it, for she had vowed to be strong and cry no more.

Then the vision would change and he was saying things that insulted her. She fled him but he seemed to come after her, calling to her to return and love him.

For a blazing moment she would be tempted, but at last came the final scene. The Duke and Lady Virginia, in Aspreys, gazing into each other's eyes as they planned for their wedding.

He must have known, even as he pursued her, that his marriage to a titled lady was inevitable and to be held soon. But that had not prevented him trying to seduce her. It was as big an insult to Lady Virginia as to herself.

In fact, she actually felt sorry for his future wife, uniting herself to a man without principle. The marriage would be a disaster and she was lucky to have escaped. She ought to be very happy.

That was when the tears began.

No sign of this appeared in her face by day. At the theatre she basked in her success, especially the first moment when Bertie had tried out the music she had written for him as Feste.

Feste was a clown, dressed in the traditional clown's motley of red and yellow. But the words of his songs tended to be sad, and the tunes Carina had written for him were gentle and sorrowful.

It had not previously occurred to her that there actually was something melancholic about Bertie. His enthusiasm, his overflowing theatricality, had all created the impression of a man with a brilliant zest for life.

Now she became aware of a sadness beneath the bonhomie. When, in Feste's character, he sang,

"Come away, come away, death,
And in sad cypress let me be laid
Fly away, fly away breath,
I am slain by a fair cruel maid."

there was a note in his voice that made her grow still, listening to him with her heart as well as her senses.

She judged him to be in his forties, although his boisterous manner often made him seem younger. So at some time he had probably been '*slain by a fair cruel maid.*'

Perhaps he was remembering that woman now, for his heart was in his song.

They were practicing at a piano backstage and when they had finished Bertie gave a little sigh and looked at her for approval.

"Is that how you meant it to sound?" he asked.

"Oh Bertie, that's beautiful. You sang as though you meant every word."

"It's the actor's art, Lady Iris. He must believe in his own heartbreak or how will the audience ever believe it?"

These days he always called her Lady Iris, as though to draw a line between her new life and her old.

"It's just that you seem to be Feste so convincingly," she said. "I remember that we discussed this once before, as we were leaving my aunt's house. You told me that you really liked playing Macbeth. Did you make yourself believe that too?"

"I didn't stab anyone, if that's what you mean. Well, I did once, but it was an accident and he was nice about it – he just stamped on my big toe in the next performance and nothing more was ever said."

Carina choked with laughter. She loved Bertie's droll reminiscences.

"No fair cruel maids?" she teased.

"Oh, my dear, dozens of them. Too many to count."

"I didn't realize you were such a Lothario."

"I'm not. I am the one who always comes off worse. Ladies dazzle me, amuse themselves with me, then drop me when they're bored."

"Stop talking nonsense," she chuckled.

"It's not nonsense." He smote his brow. "A toy, that's what I am. A plaything for the monstrous regiment of women."

He began to sing some more of Feste's lines.

"A foolish thing was but a toy,
For the rain it raineth every day."

"Well I can certainly see you as a foolish thing," Carina said.

"Ah! You mock my grief! But it's true, isn't it, that for some of us the rain '*raineth every day*'?"

His manner changed, becoming gentle.

"I know how hard it is for you. Nobody would ever suspect there was rain in your life, but it's there, isn't it? Every day."

"Yes," she sighed. "And for you too?"

He nodded.

"Do you think you will ever forget him?"

"No," Carina said softly. "I will never forget him, and I don't think I will ever stop loving him. But he's in the past now and I have a future. I am going to think about that."

"Perhaps you could learn to love someone else?" he asked hopefully.

"Not as I love him."

"But – differently? There are so many different kinds of love. Surely there could be room in your heart for another man – one day?"

Then she understood.

"Oh, Bertie," she sighed.

"It's all right, don't say anything. I know your answer would be no if you gave it now. But later perhaps, when you have had some time – I didn't even mean to tell you that I loved you, not yet.

"In fact," he continued with a touch of desperation, "I haven't really said anything, have I?"

"Not if you don't want to have said anything," she told him kindly.

"Well I don't – not yet – so I haven't. And we can go on as before, just being friends – and you don't have to think of anything – that you don't want to think of – *yes, Stanley I'm just coming.*"

He fled, leaving Carina to sit at the piano, pensive, brooding on his words.

She wondered why she had not seen it before. It seemed so obvious now.

Dear Bertie, she thought. So kind and generous. And, deep inside, such a true gentleman.

She could not give him the love he wanted. Her heart was given forever to a man who had no real use for it, except briefly.

Memory engulfed her. Against her will she relived the moment when the Duke had said,

"Place your hand over your heart, and vow to give that heart to no other man as long as you shall live."

She had given him that vow and she could not discharge it merely because he had proved treacherous. Against her will, she was bound by that promise to the end of her days.

But still, it comforted her to know that a man like Bertie lived in the real world, and that he was her loving friend.

Suddenly everything in her life was going well. The troupe relished the songs she had written for them. Even Helen was no longer hostile now that the Duke was out of their lives.

Gradually the performance was coming together.

During rehearsals Carina was fully occupied playing the piano for the singers and dancers, but she would not be needed for the actual performance, for which there was a full orchestra.

She met the conductor, who examined her music, pronounced it excellent, and allowed her to watch while he orchestrated it.

When she heard her own music played by an orchestra, Carina experienced a moment of pure heaven.

"You write very good music," he told her. "You have a real future in the theatre."

But only backstage, she thought. Soon the orchestra would be playing at the rehearsals and her part would be finished. She had a dreary vision of the others going to the theatre every evening, while she stayed behind, her job done.

But during the last rehearsal when she was scheduled to play, there was an upset during the second interval. The troupe arrived on-stage late and flustered.

"This is no good," Mr. Bentiss groaned. "Why does it always happen?"

"Because we don't have time to change our costumes," Helen said crossly. "We're on almost at the end of the second act and then we have to come on again between acts."

"Because you promised me something in the second interval," Mr. Bentiss insisted. "It's in your contract."

"But we can't do it," Helen wailed. "It's too much."

"Your contract promises me something in the second interval," Mr. Bentiss said stubbornly.

"Then let me provide it," Carina said. "I'll sing a song."

"What kind of a song?" he asked suspiciously.

"A funny song," she said at once.

"Do you know any funny songs?"

"I'll have one for you by tomorrow."

She had no idea what had made her say such a thing. But that night, sitting at the piano in the hotel, with the others crowding round, cheering her on, she wrote a funny song.

"Is there anything you can't do?" Bertie asked fervently.

"I suppose there must be lots of things Iris cannot do," Samson observed. "We just haven't found them yet!"

Everyone roared with laughter, and Carina felt a warm feeling in her heart. Their friendship and companionship meant so much to her.

Mr. Bentiss pronounced her song to be excellent. The conductor offered to orchestrate it for her, but Carina preferred to accompany herself. So it was arranged that the piano would be pushed onto the stage for her song.

At last it was the first night. The theatre was alive with

expectation, for the rumour had gone round that there was something rare and unusual about this new production.

The orchestra struck up. *Bertie's Beauties* performed their opening turn, singing a little ditty that set the scene. Then the play began.

As soon as she saw Bertie, Carina knew that he was going to be splendid. He was such a talented actor, bringing out the full measure of the clown, both the wit and the melancholy.

In the second interval Carina sang her solo and was cheered to the echo. Once again she experienced the thrill of applause that was just for her, and understood why Bertie had said she belonged in this life.

The night was a triumphant success and the party went on until the dawn. Soon all London knew that no one could truly claim to be in the fashion until they had been to the Majestic Theatre and seen *Twelfth Night*.

Carina scored a personal triumph by writing several more ditties and varying them from night to night. People began returning to see the play again, hoping to hear something new from Lady Iris.

She was the talk of the town.

*

Now the play settled in for a long run. Prosperous times had returned and Bertie felt he could indulge himself with a new suit of clothes.

He paid a visit to an establishment in Oxford Street, which he only visited when he was in funds. After an enjoyable afternoon spent being measured, selecting fabric and browsing through styles, he finally left with both his wallet and his heart lighter.

Time was getting on and he headed straight for the theatre, turning off from Oxford Street and walking briskly until he came to Hanover Square.

There he had to slow down, for the square was packed with carriages and he guessed that there must be a fashionable wedding in progress.

He began to ease himself along the street, keeping his eyes on the six great porticos of St. George's, the church where so many high society weddings took place.

People were streaming out, all dressed in the height of costly fashion. At last came the bride and groom.

The bride was a vision in white satin and lace, her veil billowing in the slight breeze, her manner triumphant.

Bertie smiled as he watched her, for he appreciated beauty of any kind.

Then he grew still as he recognised her.

It was Lady Virginia Chesterham, the young woman he had seen flirting with the Duke of Westbury at the castle, and who had become engaged to him soon afterwards, according to Carina.

So now she was the Duchess of Westbury, Bertie thought bitterly. Poor Lady Iris.

But then her bridegroom came into view, and the sight of him left Bertie thunderstruck.

Viscount Manton.

No, no, it was impossible. Manton must be the best man.

But as Bertie watched, the bridal carriage drew up, the Viscount handed Lady Virginia into it, then got in beside her.

A shower of confetti rose up in the air above them. The Viscount leaned over and kissed the bride as the carriage drew away.

There was no sign of the Duke.

Bertie began to move away, too dazed to notice where he was going.

As he walked he struggled to recall what Carina had told him.

She had seen Lady Virginia and the Duke together in Aspreys, and an assistant had told her that they were betrothed.

So the engagement had been broken off and she had swiftly contracted another one to Viscount Manton?

Or Carina had been mistaken. Maybe the Viscount had always been the intended bridegroom.

Whatever the answer, the Duke had not married her.

He quickened his pace in the direction of the theatre. He needed to see Carina without delay. She must be told this news.

But then he slowed again as a new thought came to him.

She had fled the Duke because he had only offered her illicit love, not because he was marrying another. His apparent engagement only came later.

So, in a sense, his discovery would make no difference at all.

But surely she had the right to know?

Bertie walked on, his head sunk in thought.

Carina was at the piano when he reached the theatre, experimenting with a new tune. She looked up and smiled at him.

"I think I've got it right now," she said. "Listen to this – "

"No, wait!"

"Goodness, Bertie, what's the matter. You're quite pale. Is something wrong?"

"No," he said hesitantly. "It's just – "

"Bertie dear, tell me."

Carina enclosed his hands between hers and spoke in a tone of such gentle concern that Bertie took a shuddering breath.

"It's all right," he said in a despairing voice. "You could never have loved me, could you?"

"I do love you, Bertie dear. Not in the way you want because – well, you know all about that. But as my dearest, dearest friend."

"But you could never marry me, could you?"

If Carina's ear had been quicker she might have thought he was trying to convince himself.

"I do not know," she said thoughtfully. "In a strange way, you are the only man that I could marry now."

"What?"

"I can be honest with you, because you know how things are with me. You wouldn't expect more than I can give. And in time – I don't know – "

"In time?" he breathed.

"Don't ask me that now, dear. It's too soon. Can you be a little patient?"

"If I thought I might win you in the end," he said hoarsely, "there is nothing I would not do. Nothing."

"There's no need to sound so dramatic," she said, rallying him in a teasing voice. "You won't need to do anything terrible."

"Won't I?" he asked forlornly. "Won't I?"

"Of course not. You've been listening to too much Shakespeare. All melodrama. Now, why don't you tell me what was on your mind?"

"What?"

"The thing that was troubling you."

"Oh, no – not troubling me exactly. It's just that

Stanley wants some more new songs and I thought he was putting too much pressure on you."

"But I love writing new songs and performing them. So don't worry about me. It's great fun."

"You do like this life, don't you, Iris?" He sounded almost beseeching.

Carina spoke very seriously.

"I don't know what I would have done if you hadn't stopped the coach that day, and let me catch up with you. You saved me from – well, I can't imagine what my life would have been without you. Bertie, you and I are going to reach great heights together."

"Yes, we are, aren't we?" he said, trying to smile.

"Was there anything else you wanted to tell me?"

Bertie took a deep breath.

"No, that was all."

"So everything's all right now, isn't it?"

"Yes, everything's all right," he said firmly.

But that night she was struck by something strange in his performance – a tension and a poignancy that she had never seen before.

The audience sensed it too, for the applause was extra loud for Bertie.

Carina smiled at him, delighted with his success. But he seemed strangely unwilling to meet her eyes.

She had the feeling that he was lost in another world, an unquiet place where there was no peace.

CHAPTER TEN

The year was drawing on. Summer was fading into autumn and everywhere people were making plans for the winter.

Stanley Bentiss's plans included a lavish pantomime, *Sleeping Beauty,* complete with a dream sequence, starring *Bertie's Beauties* with music by Carina.

As Bertie had predicted Melanie had married the doctor and did not return. Carina was now a fully established member of the troupe and a vital one.

Everyone recognised how much her music had contributed to their success, and they were all looking forward to the day when she and Bertie became man and wife.

There had been no fuss about their engagement. Carina had simply placed her hand gently on his arm and said, "very well, Bertie my dear. I will try to make you happy."

"And I will do everything in my power to make *you* happy," he had promised.

She knew how devotedly he loved her, enough even to accept that she could only give him half a heart, knowing that her true love had been given irrevocably to another man.

The day she promised to be his wife should have been his moment of joy, yet she still had the feeling that all was not well with Bertie. There was a haunted quality about him.

Several times she found him sitting alone, staring into space, a desperate look in his eyes.

When she touched him he would jump and she knew he had been back in the troubled world that she could not enter, that he even denied existed. Then he would give her a forced smile and start clowning.

Once she asked if he regretted their forthcoming wedding, but his denial was so vehement and his worship of her so obvious, that she never mentioned it again.

'When we are married I will make his troubles mine,' she thought. 'And I *will* be a good wife, in return for all he has given me. For I think he must be the best and kindest man in the world.

'This is my real life, not that other one. And in this life with our children, I will find all the fulfilment and satisfaction I could ask for.'

But as her wedding day approached, she would cry herself to sleep every night.

*

The first cool breezes of October were blowing when the Duke of Westbury's ship docked at Southampton where he boarded the train for London.

Four months travelling abroad had changed him. He had always been lean but now his face was almost haggard. There were shadows under his eyes from too many sleepless nights.

He seemed driven by a never ending restlessness, like a man who had sought for something for too long without success and now could find no peace.

Arriving in London, he booked into the Imperial Hotel, the most luxurious establishment in London.

"Is Your Grace seeking entertainment this evening?" the steward asked respectfully.

"Yes certainly" he replied.

He was always seeking entertainment or at least some way of passing the time that might occupy his thoughts.

But in the end there was no escaping the vision of the woman who had fled him, always just over the next horizon. Since the day she had vanished into thin air she was always just out of sight, but she never left him.

Other women passed before his eyes, but they faded before the one who lived in his mind's eye and who would not let him go.

"What entertainment is there in London tonight?" he asked wearily.

"There are many good theatrical performances, Your Grace. They say the best is *Twelfth Night* at the Majestic, but I doubt you will be able to get a ticket for that. It's the last night, and it's been sold out for a long time."

Twelfth Night. The play he had been watching on the night he was shot, when his good angel had saved his life. Perhaps it was lucky for him.

He tried to dismiss the thought as superstition, but it lingered and suddenly he found himself reaching for his wallet, pulling out a large banknote and saying,

"I am sure you can manage a miracle for me."

"Two tickets, Your Grace?"

"No, just the one. I am alone."

The steward beamed and scurried away, returning a few minutes later with a ticket for the stalls.

"I regret I was unable to secure a box for Your Grace."

"This will do very well."

In fact it suited him very well not to sit in a box, where he would have been conspicuous. He would prefer to avoid his society friends.

In his present mood he would prefer to avoid the entire

world.

At the last moment he nearly did not go to the theatre. Everything he did seemed as futile as everything else.

He thought of remaining in London for a few days or perhaps returning to his castle, but both seemed equally pointless.

He finally made up his mind at the last minute, dressed hastily in white tie and tails and leapt into the cab that the steward had summoned for him.

He reached the theatre when the rest of the audience had already gone inside and hurried to his seat as the lights went down.

There had been no time for him to consult a programme, so the immediate appearance of *Bertie's Beauties* was a shock. He scanned the girls' faces, desperately hoping for the one he knew.

Bertie had denied seeing her, but she might have returned to him later.

But she was not there.

He settled in to watch the rest of the performance, determined to seek out Bertie afterwards. He might have heard something about her.

Just before the second interval, the Duke became aware of a change in the atmosphere. A frisson of excitement swept the audience, and behind him somebody said,

"She's on next. I have seen this play three times, just for her. They say she's the cleverest woman in London, besides singing like an angel."

The Duke gave a wry smile at the word 'angel', echoing his own memories. The next moment the curtains parted, and he saw her.

She was dressed in blue satin, sparkling with silver

spangles. Everything about her was brilliant, including the assurance with which she played and sang.

The Duke felt as though a powerful shock had surged through him, paralysing his limbs.

Surely it was her. She wore no mask, but surely that was the face he had seen in the moonlight? And her voice was the one he had heard singing in a thousand dreams.

It was her!

He tried to rise in his seat, to run backstage, to seize her before she escaped, but his limbs seemed weighted. He could not move. It was part of the dream too.

In a daze he watched her, holding the audience spellbound with her wit and her music.

When she had finished the audience erupted in cheers. She curtsied, her arms opening to receive the tributes that were her due.

He knew her and he did not know her. This supremely confident creature had gone beyond him.

Perhaps that was why she had left him, because she had discovered a life that satisfied her. What could he give her that compared with this?

That thought kept him motionless in his seat when the next act started. He had been so sure of himself, what he would say to her when he found her, that suddenly he was filled with confusion.

He waited for Carina to appear again, but she did not do so until the final curtain when she lined up on-stage with all the others.

She was standing next to Bertie. To the cheers of the audience he raised her hand to his lips and kissed it gracefully.

A man behind him said,

"He's marrying her tomorrow. Lucky dog!"

The Duke rose sharply to his feet and strode from the theatre. If he had remained any longer he would have become violent.

She was marrying Bertie. But that was impossible. She was *his* wife. In his heart she had been his wife for a long time. She had promised herself to him.

In the street he stumbled away from the theatre entrance, round the corner into a side street and leaned against the wall, heaving with distress and dread.

He could not have sought her all this time, only to lose her at the last moment.

He felt the same sensation that he had experienced in the theatre, of having weights on his limbs. He stood still while the crowd emerged into the night air.

For some reason they milled around him in the side street. He could not think why they had come this way, until he realised that the stage door was nearby.

Still he did not move. His eyes were fixed on the door through which she must come.

But she was lost to him. She was to marry another man tomorrow. Now all he could do was stand and watch her walk off on Bertie's arm.

There she was, emerging from the theatre to be engulfed by the crowd. She would leave and never know that he loved her.

She was turning away. It was all over.

Suddenly he became alive again. He began to run.

"Wait! Iris, wait!"

He was sure he had cried the words aloud but no sound came out. She could not hear him. He ran out into the road, still calling.

He knew nothing of what happened next. He never saw the cab that bore down on him or heard the horse neighing with alarm, rearing in a vain attempt to avoid him.

But he felt the hoof strike his head, then the hard edge of the pavement as he fell.

The whole world was swimming. Heads crowded in above him, staring curiously as he lay there, dazed and confused and in pain.

Bertie was vaguely aware of the commotion. Leaving Carina in the centre of a happy crowd, accepting their good wishes, he ran across the road to see what had happened.

"Dear God!" he whispered when he saw who it was. "What happened?"

"It's not my fault," the cab driver was protesting. "He just dashed out in front of my horse."

"He's right," the Duke murmured weakly. "It was my fault. Just take me to my hotel. I am staying at the Imperial."

He struggled to rise and Bertie reached out to help him. The Duke's eyes seemed to clear.

"Bertie," he stammered. "Now I remember, you said you didn't know where she was. That wasn't true, was it?"

"No," Bertie admitted. "I said what she told me to say."

The Duke nodded while bells clashed in his head.

"I understand," he said weekly. "Do you love her?"

"More than anything in life."

"Take good care of her," he murmured. "Make her happy."

Bertie was white-faced. "You need a doctor," he said.

"The hotel will send for one. Please help me into the cab."

Bertie did so and stood watching as the vehicle drew away. Suddenly he could not breathe.

He walked slowly back to the stage door. Carina was waiting to get into the cab that had come for them.

"What happened?" she asked.

"Nothing," Bertie replied hoarsely. "Let's go home."

*

The whole troupe rose early next morning to prepare for the wedding. This would be no fashionable and stylish occasion. The church was just around the corner and the bride and groom would walk there together.

Carina's dress was of white silk, but plainly designed. As she put the finishing touches to her appearance, she tried not to realise that today she would be saying a final goodbye to love.

From now on her life would follow another path, one where she would devote herself to the decent, kindly man whose wife she would become in an hour's time.

"We must go now," Julia said. "Bertie's waiting for you downstairs."

Smiling, Carina kissed Julia and then the three other girls who were to be her bridesmaids. They fell in behind her and they all descended the stairs.

There Bertie stood with James, Samson and Anthony, all smartly dressed.

The sight of Bertie's face shocked her. He looked like a man suffering from a mortal illness. His skin was grey and suddenly she realised how much weight he had lost in the past few weeks.

"Come," he said, "my wife."

Side by side they walked to the little church and entered together, walking down the aisle to where the parson waited.

"*Dearly beloved –* "

As the service began, Carina felt a strong sense of

unreality. She was glad of it. It would carry her through the next half hour.

The parson addressed Bertie.

"Do you take this woman – ?"

When he had finished the long question everyone craned forward to hear Bertie's reply. They all knew how he worshipped his bride, and they were all certain that he would instantly say, "I do."

But there was silence.

As he still did not respond, Carina stared at Bertie, who now looked worse than ever.

The parson tried again.

"Do you take this woman – ?"

"No!"

Bertie's cry rang through the church, echoing out into the churchyard, so that the rooks rose into the sky, cawing madly.

"No, no, I can't!"

Bertie half turned, found the nearest pew, and collapsed into it, weeping.

"Bertie, my dear!"

Carina dropped to her knees beside him.

"Can't you tell me what is troubling you?" she begged.

"The trouble," he cried hoarsely, "is that I am a vile, dishonourable wretch. I have deceived you. I thought I could go through with it, but I cannot live with you and go on lying to you. Forgive me, forgive me."

He buried his head in his hands, sobbing as if his heart would break.

"I don't understand," she pleaded, her voice trembling.

Bertie pulled himself together.

"Come with me," he muttered.

Taking her hand he drew her to her feet and began to run out of the church. Carina scurried after him, barely able to keep up.

In the street Bertie hailed a cab and urged her aboard.

"The Imperial Hotel," he told the driver.

They sat side by side as the cab rattled along the cobbles. Bertie spoke without looking at her.

"Try not to hate me too much, although it's no more than I deserve. You said the Duke was going to marry Lady Virginia. You were wrong. She married Viscount Manton. I saw them leaving the church together. She is now Viscountess Manton."

When she did not reply, he turned to look at her.

"Don't you understand? The Duke isn't married."

"Isn't – married?" Carina whispered, struggling to keep her head against a rising tide of joy. "Are you sure?"

"He certainly did not marry Lady Virginia. I suppose he might have married someone else, but I don't think so. He was in the street outside the theatre last night. He may have been there because of you. I spoke to him after a cab had knocked him down."

"And you didn't tell me?" she cried in reproach.

"No, I didn't tell you, any more than I told you about Manton's wedding. I knew it weeks ago. I have hidden the truth from you all this time because I wanted you to marry me. Now you know how despicable I am, don't let's say any more until you have seen him."

"I am going to see him?" she gasped in disbelief, mingled with brilliant hope.

"He was taken to the Imperial Hotel last night. We are going there now."

Carina was too stunned by these revelations to fully take them in. She only knew that her world had been turned

149

upside down.

All this time Bertie had known about her mistake and had never told her. He had been going to marry her, still hiding the truth.

But at the last minute he had been unable to go through with it. He had tried to be dishonest, but he could not live with himself.

Now she understood his recent suffering. He was tormented by what he had done.

When she could speak it was to stutter,

"As you say – he may yet be married – to someone else. He did not want to marry me."

"When you see him," he said raggedly, "he will tell you what he wants."

She clasped and unclasped her hands. To see him again after all this time. She must try to stay calm, not to hope for too much. Nothing had really changed, unless – had he really come to the theatre last night to see her?

At the hotel Bertie helped her down from the cab and together they walked into the foyer of the grandiose establishment. The man on the reception desk stared at them. Suddenly Carina realised what a sight they must present, running about London in bridal clothes.

"I must see the Duke of Westbury without delay," Bertie commanded.

"His Grace cannot see anyone," the receptionist declared. "He is dying."

Carina gasped and buried her face in her hands.

"I know he was injured last night," Bertie said. "I saw him just after he had been knocked down, but he told me he wasn't badly hurt. He got to his feet and returned to this hotel."

"Indeed he did," the man said, thawing a little at

Bertie's evident knowledge of the situation. "But when he reached here, he collapsed. We sent for a doctor to attend to his injuries, but he developed a fever and has become delirious. He calls constantly for his wife."

Carina's heart lurched. Her world turned to darkness again.

"But nobody has ever heard of there being a Duchess," the receptionist continued. "His marriage was not reported in the newspapers."

"It hasn't taken place yet," Bertie said. "Now, allow me take this lady upstairs to see him. You'll find that this will solve the problem."

The receptionist seemed too bemused to question them any further and they ran up the stairs without hindrance.

At the door of the grand suite they paused. Carina was trying to pluck up courage, desperately praying that the Duke would not die.

As soon as they pushed open the door, they heard him calling feverishly,

"Call for my wife – fetch my wife – I saw her last night – tell her she must come to me – she promised – always – but then she left me – find her – please tell her – "

"He means you," Bertie said. "Hurry now."

Carina was already speeding across the floor to throw herself on her knees beside the Duke's bed.

"I am here, my darling, I am here. Look at me. Did you think I would not come?"

The Duke grasped her with feverish hands, staring wildly into her face.

"You!" he said hoarsely. "Are you a dream?"

"No, my dearest, I am no dream. I am here and I am yours. Feel me."

She took his hands in hers and then clasped her arms

around him, holding him against her heart in a protective embrace of deep affection.

Bertie, watching them, covered his eyes.

"I told them you would come," the Duke murmured, "but they did not believe me. They think I have no wife, but it's you – "

Then his mind seemed to clear and he became aware of her bridal gown. She saw the dread in his eyes and hastened to ease his mind.

"I am not married," she said. "I might have been, but it has been called off. Truly, I am not married."

"Then our wedding must take place as soon as possible," he said urgently. "And you will become my wife in the eyes of the world, as well as in my heart and soul"

"Everything shall be as you wish," Carina promised. "But rest now. You need to get well."

"I dare not close my eyes, in case you vanish."

"I shall never leave you again," she vowed solemnly.

Gradually he relaxed his grip on her hand and lay back on the pillows. But his eyes remained on her face until they closed.

At once Carina went around the side of the bed to where the doctor had been standing back, watching.

"Tell me how bad he is," she begged. "They said downstairs that he was dying – "

"Oh no, no, it's not as bad as that. Rumours grow every time they are passed on. It's true he collapsed when he arrived back here last night and he has been feverish, but nothing to cause undue alarm."

He smiled at her kindly.

"And now I think he has taken a medicine better than any I can give him."

He left soon after, giving her instructions as to what

medication to give to the Duke and when.

She sat by his sleeping figure, still not fully understanding what had happened, but knowing that he loved and needed her and that they would never be parted again.

For the moment that was all she needed to know.

At last the Duke's valet approached her.

"The gentleman who came with you is outside in the corridor. He wants to know what you wish him to do."

"Ask him to come in, please."

Poor Bertie, she thought. Whatever wrong he may have done, she could not bring herself to be angry with him. His conscience had punished him far more deeply than anything else. And at last, he had restored her to her loved one.

Her heart poured out to him as he came slowly into the room. She ran to him at once, taking his hand and drawing him into a corner.

"Dear Bertie," she said.

"Don't be kind to me," he said miserably. "I don't deserve it."

"You have always been my best friend," she said. "And I shall never forget that."

"I lied to you. I was going to marry you with a lie."

"But you didn't. You couldn't do it, because you really are the good man I always believed in."

"No, I am a man who loves you. I shall never say that to you again, but it's true. I suddenly saw what I was doing and I was horrified at myself. I only want you to be happy."

"I will be, thanks to you. Thank you for bringing me back to him."

Bertie sighed.

"I suppose that's the end of Lady Iris."

"Well, it's the end of my performing career, but I have written all the music for the pantomime. That's yours now. And later – well, who knows what else I may write."

"Promise that you'll bring your next composition to me and nobody else."

"Of course."

He kissed her hand one last time.

"Be happy, Lady Iris," he said. "May it never rain for you."

There was a restless movement from the bed and Carina turned quickly. Bertie saw that she had forgotten him completely.

"I'll go now," he said.

"Goodbye, Bertie dear."

She gave him a brief kiss on the cheek and ran straight back to the bed. Bertie saw her kneel down, stretching out her arms to the man she loved.

He touched his cheek where she had kissed it.

Then he slipped away, unnoticed by either of them.

In the corridor he paused and his eyes filled with tears, as he tried to summon enough courage to go back to the world.

*

"What is it, my darling?" Carina whispered.

The Duke was staring up at her face, almost as though he had never seen her before.

"It was you, wasn't it?" he murmured. *"Twelfth Night.* All those years ago. The little girl in the next box, who saved my life. You held me in your arms then, just as you are doing now."

"Yes, it was me," she said tenderly.

"And your name is Carina. You told me that all those years ago. And I told you that it meant beloved. You have been my beloved ever since.

"In my heart my beloved has never left me and when I met Lady Iris I knew that she too would never leave me. I believe that secretly I knew that both of you were the same woman.

"You both came to save me. When we met a few months ago, I was a despicable man – arrogant, selfish and careless of everything except my own pleasure.

"I saw you and wanted you. I thought I could have you for the asking – no, the demanding. I believed it would be that easy.

"I thought I could buy your true love with jewels and luxury and in my intolerable pride I assumed the right to make you my mistress. You showed me what you thought of me and you were right. You fled me because I was not worthy of you."

She bent and kissed him.

"I fled you because I loved you so much that I was tempted to stay with you on any terms," she said. "But I knew I must not become your mistress and be despised by you in the end."

"I could never despise you," he vowed. Then he sighed. "But your true value was something I had to learn. I have searched for you high and low. I visited Bertie in London, but he denied knowing where you were you. He said you told him to."

"I did. I saw you in Aspreys with Lady Virginia."

"You were there?"

"I came to the door and saw you together. I didn't see Viscount Manton."

"He was deep inside the shop. I was with the pair of

them, buying a wedding gift."

"And I thought that you and she – "

"Never in this life," he said so forcefully that he began to cough.

He coughed until he was tired and she laid him down and gave him some medicine.

When he was somewhat recovered he said,

"I went abroad soon after. On my way back through Europe, I joined them for a couple of days in Paris. I can only say that I'm sorry for Manton. I could not have married Virginia for all the tea in China!"

He looked at her.

"If you had known the truth, we might have found each other then."

"No," she said thoughtfully. "It was too soon. I had a lot to learn about myself, things that I am glad to have discovered."

"Like what a star performer you are? Will you think me a very heavy-handed husband if I say that a Duchess cannot perform on the stage?"

"I have no desire to perform on a stage. My place is behind the scenes, writing music. I have promised Bertie all my future compositions. And I think there will probably be a great many of them."

She looked at him, a hint of challenge in her eyes.

"I am going to have to give in on this one, aren't I, my dearest?" he said warily.

Smiling, she nodded.

"Then we need discuss it no further," he said. "Except that you must tell me under what name these compositions will be played."

"I promise not to drag the name of Westbury into the theatre."

"My darling, I am trying, not very subtly, to discover your name. Do you realise that, although we are engaged to be married, I do not know what your real name is. I know your first name is Carina, but not your family name."

"It is Denton. Miss Carina Denton. I own a small property in Worcestershire, and enough money to be comfortably independent, but that is all. I have no great title or standing in society."

"I care nothing for any of that. I only care for you. Do you remember that I once asked you to place your hand over your heart, and vow to give that heart to no other man as long as you lived?"

"I remember."

"And you did," he reminded her. "You said, 'no man but you, all my life.' And I told you that no power on earth could take my heart from you.

"My darling girl, I must tell you that is as true now as it was then and it will be true all our lives. I shall spend the rest of my days making up to you for the wrong I did you, that so nearly caused us to lose each other."

He drew her into his arms and kissed her fervently. Even through his weakness she could feel the passion she had sensed in the castle garden, and which could command her own passion in return.

For the first time she was truly free to love him and be loved by him, with no shadows between them.

When he released her, she held his face between her hands and said softly and lovingly,

"I will spend the rest of my days loving you and making you happy. Oh, my darling! We took such winding paths to find each other. But from now on there is only one path and it leads us both to Heaven."